THE PRIVATE APARTMENTS

STORIES

IDMAN NUR OMAR

Published in Canada and the USA in 2023 by House of Anansi Press Inc.
houseofanansi.com

House of Anansi Press is committed to protecting our natural environment.
This book is made of material from well-managed FSC®-certified forests, recycled materials,
and other controlled sources.   .

House of Anansi Press is a Global Certified Accessible™ (GCA by Benetech) publisher.
The ebook version of this book meets stringent accessibility standards and is available
to readers with print disabilities.

27 26 25 24 23   1 2 3 4 5

Library and Archives Canada Cataloguing in Publication
Title: The private apartments : stories / Idman Nur Omar.
Names: Omar, Idman Nur, author.
Identifiers: Canadiana (print) 20220414815 | Canadiana (ebook) 20220414858 |
ISBN 9781487011383 (softcover) | ISBN 9781487011390 (EPUB)
Classification: LCC PS8629.M315 P75 2023 | DDC C813/.6—dc23

Cover design: Alysia Shewchuk
Cover image: (apartment building) Anhenaridita / Shutterstock.com
Text design and typesetting: Lucia Kim

*House of Anansi Press is grateful for the privilege to work on and create from the Traditional Territory
of many Nations, including the Anishinabeg, the Wendat, and the Haudenosaunee, as well as the Treaty
Lands of the Mississaugas of the Credit.*

With the participation of the Government of Canada
Avec la participation du gouvernement du Canada

*We acknowledge for their financial support of our publishing program the Canada Council for the Arts,
the Ontario Arts Council, and the Government of Canada.*

Printed and bound in Canada

MIX
Paper from
responsible sources
FSC
www.fsc.org   FSC® C103567

Advance Praise for *The Private Apartments*

"Idman Nur Omar's stories have a prismatic and glittering brilliance. *The Private Apartments* spans the world, tracing the passageways that join one life to another in writing that is wise, clear-eyed, and bold. This astonishing collection heralds a major new talent."

—Madeleine Thien, author of *Do Not Say We Have Nothing*

"The closely observed characters in these stories amount to a poignant work of short fiction that could also be called a novel. Idman Omar's light touch insightfully connects the start of the 1991 Somali Civil War with the forms of life that grow from uprootedness and struggle into lasting shape elsewhere. This work, spanning continents and two decades, reveals a writer of incisive narrative vulnerability and asks us to read her intimate graces as a storyteller with mature tenderness. The distinctive pleasures of *The Private Apartment*'s stories are waiting. Why not come in?"

—Canisia Lubrin, author of *Code Noir*

"*The Private Apartments* absorbed me from the very beginning. Idman Nur Omar is a skilled writer, whose sensitive and stirring depiction of the lives of Somali immigrants calls to mind Jhumpa Lahiri's *Interpreter of Maladies*. I cared about these characters. I felt curious about them, gutted for them. I kept reading as much for the crisp, graceful writing and complicated, human portraits as to see what would happen next."

—Shashi Bhat, author of *The Most Precious Substance on Earth*

"*The Private Apartments* invites you into the secret lives of Somali women who dare to migrate towards safety, solitude, and sometimes joy. It suggests that even across oceans, behind closed doors, and in every corner of every room, someone, somewhere is boldly (read: messily) giving life another shot. Idman Nur Omar is cool and delicate on a prose level and generous in her belief that your neighbour is actually your friend, your sibling, your cousin, and the person you come home to. There is almost nothing private about being this intimately connected. I mourn for these women; I feel their guilt and pleasures as much as I celebrate them, as they are, in many strange and uncomfortably daring ways, versions of myself."

— Téa Mutonji, author of *Shut Up You're Pretty*

"Idman Nur Omar's remarkable debut tells stories of Somalis in the diaspora as they navigate complicated relationships, loss, and displacement with determination and wit. Omar writes with sensitivity, insight, and quiet assurance. The voices in these stories are sharp, vulnerable, and, at times, brash. A delightful read!"

— Djamila Ibrahim, author of *Things Are Good Now*

For my mother

But your image is before me all the time.
Like the spirit of someone I have wronged.
And yet, I have not wronged you, have I?
—Ama Ata Aidoo, *Our Sister Killjoy*

Contents

Rome, 1991

I DISLIKED VISITING Aunt Nina. She was twenty-two years older than my mother: a half-sibling from my grandfather's first marriage. My mother and my aunt were never close, and back then, we hardly saw her. Aunt Nina was running her real estate company and selling properties across the Lazio region. She reappeared in my life at that pivotal time when I had to decide whether to attend college or start working full-time with my father at his auto repair shop. She asked about my interests, and after some consideration, I said architecture. My answer seemed to please her, and she promised to pay my tuition if I maintained good grades. She even arranged an internship for me at a commercial development company and, once I graduated, organized job interviews with some of her contacts. I was grateful to her, so I forced myself to visit, even though she kept me for hours.

I was at work when one of the secretaries found me in the supply room and told me there was a call waiting for me. Aunt Nina was on the phone, telling me to come over after work. I knew it was a pretext to have me stay for dinner, but she claimed she had hired a new housekeeper she wanted me to meet. I left my car in its parking space at work and walked the few blocks to my aunt's apartment. I was irritated that she had called on me for this purpose and that I was obligated to accommodate her. She had mentioned that her housekeeper was a refugee from Somalia. The moral gravity in her voice made my light, distracted tone seem like I was either uninformed or uninterested in the war. I knew about it, of course — there was occasional coverage in the papers, accompanied by a photo of some collapsed, bullet-ridden building or a group of wide-eyed, skinny Black children staring straight into the camera lens. I also noticed the increasing number of Africans in the city. Just the week before, I had bumped into one while getting onto the train at Termini. I apologized instinctively, and he turned to me, smiling with big, jagged teeth, and replied in perfect Italian, "These things happen on crowded trains."

It was Ladan who came to the door of Aunt Nina's apartment, and, for a brief moment, I felt bizarrely out of place — as though I had knocked on the wrong door or had come to meet some other refugee girl, because she could not have been the one my aunt had mentioned. Ladan was tall and shapely, with soft features that wore a severe expression. I was at a loss for words, and I could barely look at her she was so beautiful.

"Raffael?" she said, moving aside to let me in.

I became embarrassed that she called me by my name; I could do little more than nod and rush off to the great room where Aunt Nina was sitting in her armchair. I bent over to kiss her and sat on the sofa. My aunt was watching one of her soap operas; I stared ahead at the television, feigning interest. Ladan took a seat on the opposite end of the sofa.

"Well, this is Ladan!" my aunt said. She pronounced her name La-*danne*.

I turned my head to look at her again. Her hair was dark and frizzy, worn in a bun, and I had the impression of a mole somewhere on her face. I quickly looked away.

"Nice to meet you," she said.

"The pleasure is mine."

"Her Italian is good, no?" my aunt said.

"Yes, very good. Where did you learn?"

"Her father was educated in Italian," my aunt answered. "He taught her and her brother."

"Ah, I see. How long have you been in Rome?" I asked.

"Almost a year," Ladan said. "Should I make coffee?"

Her manner was somewhat austere, like she was conscious of making a good impression, though for what, she did not know. She reminded me of a grade school teacher. Those young women who are very stern with children. I thought she would make a lovely mother.

I began to visit my aunt's apartment almost every day after work. Aunt Nina was happy enough to see me, and Ladan grew to expect me. I knew this because when I followed her to the kitchen, she had three cups already set out on the tray. Occasionally, my aunt would bake a pound cake, and we would enjoy it together in front of the television. If my talking with Ladan distracted my aunt from her soap opera, she would shoo us away and I would carry our drinks and dessert to the dining table, where I could almost pretend we were alone. She would often recount the chores she had finished or the errands she had run that day, as though my family had sent me to keep a watchful eye over her. The first few times, I interrupted, hushing her by clicking my tongue. But then I realized she hardly spoke outside of this, besides asking me generic questions about my family and work. I began to listen, just to hear her talk, and ask questions of my own. *Was the grocery store busy? Is my aunt difficult? Do you always mix vinegar and baking soda to clean the refrigerator?* Sometimes she would answer me earnestly, in her soft, direct tone. Other times she would stare at me strangely, like she could not understand why I had such an interest in her cleaning methods. I thought about her all day, counting the hours at work until I could see her. I felt oddly protective and insecure, like I was coveting a close friend's little sister; she was nineteen, and I was twenty-six.

Then, one Friday afternoon, my colleagues and I had a small surprise party in the office on my boss's birthday, and he was in such a good mood, he declared the workday over. I headed over to my aunt's apartment early, and while climbing the stairs, I heard Ladan on the second floor landing, arguing with a male voice I couldn't identify. The man was asking her repeatedly if she was sure about something. I came upon them as naturally as I could, and it seemed like perfect timing, because Ladan pointed at me and said, "Ask him. Do you know him? He's her nephew."

The man was Bruno Costa, a pilot for Alitalia and my aunt's downstairs neighbour. He was in his late forties — twice divorced, with teenage children who never visited him. I knew all of this because my aunt had relayed his history, quite sarcastically, after we passed him in front of his door one evening. Right away, I could tell that Bruno had no interest in asking me anything.

"That's all right," he said, making a casual, swatting motion with his hand, his gaze holding Ladan's. "I believe you now."

Ladan looked annoyed, but she carried on up the stairs without another word. She put away my aunt's dry cleaning, and I paced around the hallway. Finally, I pulled Ladan's elbow and drew her into the study.

"Be careful," I told her.

"Be careful of what?" Ladan asked, already looking alarmed.

"Never mind," I said, getting the sense that I was overreacting. "Just tell me if he bothers you again, okay?"

Ladan seemed touched by my concern. She nodded, smiling.

A few days later, I found Ladan in the kitchen, washing up at the sink. She was wearing a dress my aunt had bought her as a gift. It was pale yellow with a floral pattern, fitted close to her waist, and then stopped at her calves. She greeted me casually with her back turned. Her neck was bent forward, and her hair had become loose in its ponytail, with tight black curls sweeping her shoulders. I did not think of my aunt in the other room. I did not think at all. I moved towards her instinctively and hugged her from behind, resting my chin on her shoulder and wrapping my arms around hers. To feel her body against mine gave me such pleasure that I pulled her closer and inhaled the coconut scent of her neck, dropping my hands into the soapy water to find hers.

Ladan jerked away fiercely, causing me to stumble backwards, and turned to face me. She squinted at me, her mouth partly open. I had never seen her angry.

"I—I'm sorry," I started weakly. "I just—Ladan, I—"

"I'm working," she said.

"Right, yes. I know."

"And you're not my husband," she said. "You have no right to touch me."

I backed out of the room, made some excuse to my aunt, and left awkwardly. I stayed away for weeks after that, unsure of what, exactly, I had ruined.

WINTER SET IN and I learned that Aunt Nina had become sick. While clearing the dinner table, my mother asked me if I was intent on making her seem like a bad sister. My aunt had called her, coughing into the phone. I explained that I hadn't been visiting my aunt as usual since I had been assigned to a big project. My mother decided we would visit Aunt Nina together that Sunday. Even though I was not prepared to face Ladan—I was still thinking of ways to make it up to her—I now had a legitimate reason to visit my aunt. I hoped seeing Ladan again in more sombre circumstances would be enough to break the ice between us.

When we arrived at my aunt's apartment, Ladan wouldn't look at me. She took the two containers of soup my mother had prepared and nodded towards the bedroom where my aunt was resting. I sat in a chair next to my aunt while my mother perched on the bed.

"Has work kept you so busy?" my aunt asked me in her new raspy voice. "We've missed you."

I promised to visit more. I kept thinking of how to begin my apology to Ladan, which words to use, but I couldn't even mumble a goodbye when it was time to leave.

By chance, I saw her on the street some days later. She was wearing jeans and a red men's winter coat. She looked as though she was waiting for someone, and soon, a thin man with an Afro approached her. He was only in a sweater, and I knew right away that he was Ladan's brother and that she wore his jacket. I stood watching, backing into the front of the deli where I had just purchased a sandwich. Ladan reached into her pocket and handed her brother an envelope, which he tore open and threw to the ground. She stepped back as he started counting cash. It was only then that I noticed they were in front of a bank. He moved closer to her, holding the folded money between their faces. For a moment, I was sure he would hit her. I went to cross the road but was stopped short by a car horn. I had to wait for two more cars to pass, but by then Ladan was back inside the bank. She returned minutes later with more cash, but she hadn't put it in an envelope this time; she pushed the money into her brother's chest and walked hurriedly down the street. He stood there, holding the money to his heart.

~

I RETURNED TO my aunt's apartment that evening. It took some time for anyone to come to the door, and I was surprised when it was my aunt, a blanket draped over her shoulders, who let me in.

"Oh, good," she said. "Come, come." She led me to the sitting room, where Ladan was also wrapped in a blanket. She was sitting on the hardwood floor, leaning against the sofa, sobbing. She turned away as soon as she saw me.

"What's wrong?" I said, sitting across from her.

Ladan wouldn't talk to me.

"Now, now, La-danne. Let's not keep secrets. Raffael is your friend," my aunt said conspiratorially.

"I have no friends," Ladan said under her breath.

"That's not true! *We* are your friends. Isn't that right, Raffael?" My aunt looked at me and added, "Her brother is mistreating her."

"Signora!" Ladan shot my aunt a look of outrage. Aunt Nina meekly raised her hands in apology.

"I saw you," I said. "In front of Banco di Roma. Was that your brother?"

Ladan stared at me with an amazed expression.

"I know he takes your money," I said matter-of-factly, even though I was afraid. I had the impression that I was wandering blindly on dangerous terrain. That I was being presumptuous about a relationship I knew very little about, and that Ladan could write me off for good because of it.

But her eyes widened, as if I had rightly hit upon a sore nerve, thereby unlocking all of her resentment.

"He takes *everything*," she said, as if to correct me. "Everything. And he does nothing. He doesn't work. Not outside, not at home. He sits at the terminal all day with his friends — even though his wife is pregnant and needs help."

We were all quiet for a while.

"He acts like he brought me here." Ladan looked at my aunt and then at me. "He didn't bring me here! My father arranged it. Right before he was killed. He had a contact at the embassy, and he left us money. My father paid for our visas and our passports and everything. My brother didn't bring me here! I don't owe him anything!"

She had worked herself up and was trying to control her emotions. She looked frail and pitiful. I felt for the first time that my infatuation, my attraction to her, was something much deeper. That ours was a divine meeting in which I was meant to protect her.

"Okay, that's enough," my aunt said. "Get some rest, La-danne. I put a nightdress on the bed for you. Come now." My aunt stood up slowly and reached for Ladan's hand. She walked Ladan to the hallway and came back. I heard the guest bedroom door close. "She's been like that all day."

I shook my head and took off my loose tie.

"Did you really see her? At the bank?"

"Yes, just in front of it."

"She gave him money?"

"He takes her earnings! Clearly." I was angry. Angrier now than when I had witnessed the exchange.

"That's terrible. I pay her well, you know."

"I hate it," I said.

"Poor thing. She'll have to manage."

"How?" I asked.

"I managed. Look at me. I made something out of nothing. Besides, she's young. And she's pretty. I wouldn't be surprised if one of these old bachelors tries to marry her."

"That's ridiculous," I said.

"What do you mean? Signor Costa finds any reason to knock on my door these days. I can tell from the way he looks at her, you know." My aunt laughed. "He's been divorced for ten years and he's sworn off marriage. Can you imagine? Signor Costa with a Black wife thirty years his junior!"

I was rubbing my face to distract myself from the thought of some old man seizing such an opportunity. "She wouldn't do that," I said, hoping my expression didn't betray my jealousy.

My aunt must have thought I was challenging her. She became serious. "Don't be stupid, Raffael. She wouldn't do that? A nice home like this? No need to work and look after an old woman like me? Freedom from her brother? Let me tell you something, Raffael, she would welcome it!"

I saw that my aunt meant every word, and it felt like an ominous warning, like a piece of unsolicited but gravely needed advice. For a second, I wondered if Aunt Nina could see past the innocence of my visits the same way she saw past Signor Costa's.

It didn't matter. The circumstances had changed. I knew in that moment that Ladan would forgive me. She would accept me and love me, and be grateful to me. It seemed to me then that my whole purpose in life was geared towards her.

"I'm going to marry her," I said.

"What was that?" My aunt was looking for the TV remote behind the cushions of the sofa.

"I'm going to marry Ladan."

"A BLACK GIRL? You're going to let him marry a Black girl?" We were at my family home, and Aunt Nina was standing and pointing at Ladan. My parents were trying their best to calm my aunt as she accused Ladan of plotting to seduce me.

Ladan said nothing, listening to my aunt's accusations with a puzzled expression. Finally, I took Ladan by the hand and escorted her out of the house. We walked briskly and in silence, me gripping her hand tight, until we came to a park.

I apologized to Ladan on behalf of my aunt. "I don't

think like that," I said. "I want you to know." I was embarrassed and out of breath.

"That's okay," she said, picking up a twig from the ground.

"No, it isn't." My aunt knew Ladan and liked her. She had said countless times that she would have loved a daughter like Ladan. The last thing I wanted was for Ladan to feel unwelcome, to second-guess her decision to marry me. "I love you," I said. "I don't care that you're Black."

Ladan seemed amused. "Raffael," she began, "do you think if my parents were here — if my parents were alive — that they would accept *you*? Your aunt is not the only one who is disappointed," she said, as though pointing out an obvious fact. "My brother won't even speak to me."

"Yes, well, you don't need him," I said.

"He's still my brother." She threw the twig she was holding.

I rubbed my face roughly. Already, I was blaming Aunt Nina for introducing me to this girl who always managed to elude me, for igniting my jealousy and inspiring my hasty proposal with her theories about her neighbour, and for causing a scene in front of Ladan and my parents. I felt that everything was hanging in the balance. I didn't know where we would stand in the next few moments. I could feel my ears becoming red. I continued to rub my face in an acute state of agony, but then I felt Ladan's hand on top of mine.

"Stop." She pulled my hand away from my face and held it between us. "Let's not worry about it."

We wed that spring in the garden of a renovated villa belonging to Aunt Nina's good friend Silvio Rochetti. Ladan couldn't be persuaded to go near a church, but she allowed a priest to marry us after I pleaded with her. It was a small wedding, with mostly my family and some friends. We danced and ate cake and listened to the speeches of my family, including Aunt Nina, who seemed resigned and weary. Only Ladan's sister-in-law came, holding her newborn daughter and congratulating us in broken Italian. I watched as they sat on a bench, Ladan taking the small baby in her arms. She looked preoccupied, like she was trying to think over the chatter, laughter, and celebratory exclamations of the guests. Even the baby seemed less disoriented than her. But I was truly happy. The best possible outcome had been achieved for both Ladan and me.

London, 1998

WARDA REACHED OUT her arm and felt the coolness of the sheets around her. She opened her eyes. He wasn't there. She became aware of the home phone ringing faintly in the sitting room. She thought, irritation surfacing, that it was Daud calling to explain where he was. He had stayed out late only once before — in the early days of their marriage — and Warda's best friend, Filsun, had advised her to put her foot down. She may have gone a little too far with her threats, because Daud, whom she had never seen enraged, seemingly lost control of himself and began breaking the furniture in the living room. But Warda wasn't frightened — rather, she was baffled that someone would destroy their own property. She made him go out and buy a new television and end table the next day.

The phone continued to ring. Warda looked at the alarm clock on Daud's nightstand: it was just past three a.m. She rose to answer the call.

"Hello?"

"Warda? Warda! Oh my God." It was Filsun. "I've been calling you all night! Why haven't you answered? Oh my God, I was so —"

"I was sleeping. What's wrong?" Warda's first thought was of Daud.

"Are you okay? Is everything okay?"

"Yes. I'm fine. Why?"

"I was just worried. Listen, where's Daud?"

"He's not here," Warda said.

"Oh. He hasn't come home yet?"

"No. Why?"

"I don't want to scare you, but something's happened."

"What happened? Is he okay?"

"He got into a fight. Not a fight, exactly. Almost — he almost —"

"He almost got into a fi —?"

"Warda! With Yusuf."

Warda looked at the front door.

"Warda!"

"Yes, I heard you."

"My husband was there. They were at that Turkish restaurant, and then Yusuf came and sat next to Daud.

16

Yusuf whispered something to him, and they walked out together."

"They don't know each other," Warda said defensively.

"What if they do?"

"No, Filsun. Trust me, they don't know each other. I've never spoken to Daud about—"

"Warda! They got up and walked out together! My husband saw. And he followed them because he knows Daud's crazy."

"That's why."

"Yes. I mean, no offence, but he does have a history—"

"That's why he didn't come home," Warda said, mostly to herself.

"Heh?"

"So did he hit him? Did Daud hit him?"

"No, no. See, Ahmed knew something might happen. He walked out after them and stood around, but then he saw a police car go by, and he didn't want to take any chances."

"So... he didn't."

"No, it didn't get that far, thank God." Filsun sighed. "But listen. Ahmed was pulling Daud away, right? And he heard him say to Yusuf, very serious, 'She doesn't have it.' Warda, why would he say that?"

Warda massaged her neck. "I don't know."

"What is he talking about?"

"I told you, I don't know."

Filsun breathed heavily into the phone. "He must still be looking for that gold."

Warda didn't say anything.

"You have to come here. Take a cab, or I can send Ahmed to pick you up. I'm sorry, but I don't trust Daud. Remember the time he broke your TV?"

"He won't break the TV. It's new."

"Warda, I don't trust him. I don't."

Warda laughed. "He's not a dangerous person." She stretched out on the sofa and yawned. "When did your husband get home?"

"Two hours ago now."

"Hm."

"Maybe," Filsun started, "he did tell Ahmed that he knew someone. Yusuf's cousin, or his tribesman or something. I think Daud's trying to figure it out."

"Filsun." Warda sat up decisively. She wanted to end the conversation. "It's probably just a misunderstanding. I'll talk to him."

"Misunderstanding? Men aren't like that. If he even thinks Yusuf—"

"I don't care about Yusuf!" Warda snapped. "I don't want to hear his name!"

"Okay, okay."

"He has nothing! No money, no car, no nothing! Let alone gold. Are you joking?"

"Okay. Fine."

Warda exhaled loudly. She was annoyed that Filsun knew so much and felt the right to meddle in her relationship.

"Just—if you're not going to come here, then at least call me. If he comes home or anything. You'll call me, right?"

"Mhmm."

"Just call me."

"I will."

But Warda wouldn't call Filsun back, nor would she divulge any details about what happened that morning when Daud returned. She believed, above all else, that marriage was between two people, and that good or bad, Daud was hers to deal with.

IN THEIR BEDROOM, opposite the window, was a large wardrobe that took up most of the wall. On the upper shelf there were two shoeboxes stacked on top of each other. The first box was slim and held important documents: Warda's certificate of naturalization, immunization records, appliance warranties. There were a few old photos in this box as well—photos that were taken after she had first arrived in England. She looked thin and gawky, her eyes almost too big for the rest of her face. In all of the pictures, she was sitting on the floor, holding one of her uncle's babies, or standing in the background, grinning stupidly. She was thirteen then, though her papers stated she was eleven.

When she was seventeen, she started attending weddings with her uncle's wife, who would lend Warda a diraac, usually something plain or outdated that she herself would not wear or had already worn numerous times. But Warda, with her slim figure and youth, would manage, even in her inexperience, to look elegant and understated. She was eager to get out of the flat and accompany her aunt to these functions. To see the women she had only heard about through gossip, with dyed red or blond hair and chunky jewellery, sitting at tables or standing near entryways, their hands clasped, always appearing slightly disappointed. Warda would leave the banquet hall and step outside for fresh air, where she would inevitably run into a groomsman or a male guest who was smoking or giving parking directions. These men were older than her, and they acted so captivated by Warda it surprised her—how willing they were to give her things.

Ilyas had been the first; he bought her a mobile phone—though he stopped paying the bill when he heard she used it to talk to other men. Omar had taught her how to drive, and when she had obtained her driver's licence, he lent her his silver Peugeot from time to time. Ali had paid for her favourite fur-lined, calf-length winter coat. It was so expensive that she ripped up the receipt when the cashier handed it to her, out of fear that her aunt would find it and question her about where she got the money for such a purchase; however, Warda didn't feel the least bit guilty. She felt like a dam had broken. She had spent so many years with so few personal belongings, afraid to ask her uncle for anything because he was always tired and burdened from driving his truck. He had already done so much for her simply by bringing her to the U.K., so Warda would take whatever was offered.

But Yusuf had nothing to give. Warda asked herself why Filsun had introduced her to him in the first place. Yusuf lived with his older sister, Nasra, whom Warda had seen from afar at weddings. He had been laid off from his factory job, and for six months, he would collect unemployment benefits. Warda knew not to expect anything from him then, but she found that Yusuf was easy to talk to precisely because she did not care what he thought of her. If she rebuffed or ignored him, he carried on just the same as though it had never happened. He orchestrated ways to be near her. To bump into her in her neighbourhood, to see her, even if only briefly. Warda obliged once in a while, until, one day, while they walked side by side, he reached out and picked a leaf off a tree. He handed the leaf to her.

"Here," he said, grinning, "pretend it's a flower."

Warda stopped abruptly and looked at his outstretched hand. "It's not a flower," she said. Yusuf quickly let the leaf go, and Warda watched it flutter to the pavement. "Even if it was," she added, resuming her stride, "I would have no use for it."

Around that time, Daud entered her life so subtly, so gradually, that Warda could not recall exactly how their acquaintance had begun. Only that she threw her cousins out of their shared bedroom in the evenings so she could talk to him on the phone in private. He had his own flat, a new car, and a good job working construction. He was not the first man to mention marriage to her, but he was the first one whose sincerity seemed actionable, rather than just flattering and wishful.

ONE NIGHT, WARDA murmured goodbye to Daud, hung up her mobile phone, and glanced around the bedroom. The girls' bunk beds were to her left, with their unmade pink and purple checkered bedding, and their colouring books and markers were strewn across the carpet. Warda would have to clean it up. For the first time, she asked herself why she was still there. Why was she—at twenty-one—still sharing a bedroom with *children*? Why was she getting them prepared for school in the morning and waiting for them by the gates in the afternoon, when she *herself* was mostly kept out of school by her aunt in order to help raise them? Why was she in the kitchen every day at four p.m. to start cooking a meal that her aunt had decided on? The air in the room had suddenly thickened. Warda wanted nothing more than to escape that room and that flat. To escape the chores and duties that awaited her every day. The hungry eyes and pressing needs of her little cousins. The entitled demands of her aunt and the exhausted indifference of her uncle.

Daud asked for her hand a month later. And although many people called Warda to congratulate her, including the men she had briefly dated, Yusuf was incredulous. She ignored his calls for a while, finally picking up so she could be rid of him. She told him that it was true. That she was getting married and that he shouldn't call her anymore. He sounded taken aback, as if he had secretly hoped for her to deny the rumours and reassure him.

A week later, he called to tell her he had gotten a job. A week after that, he asked her to meet him. Warda refused at first, but Yusuf said he wanted to give her something really important. They met in the food court of the shopping centre near her uncle's flat. Warda was afraid that someone might see her. She was afraid that she would have to explain all of it to Daud, who wouldn't understand. Yet she was also secretly pleased because she had not realized how deeply she could affect someone. She knew that Yusuf was trying to prove something to her. He looked solemn when she approached him. He didn't stand up or even greet her when she sat down. He asked her some questions that she thought were meant to gauge the seriousness of her engagement.

He looked at her hand. "No ring?" he asked.

She brushed her ring finger. "What are we, gaalo? That's not our culture."

"What about gold? Did he bring you any gold?"

He hadn't, but Warda didn't want to admit this. Daud had brought a thousand pounds when he came to her uncle's house to ask for her hand, and it was promptly distributed among the party. They were going to have a wedding and buy new furniture, and he was giving her a small dowry, too. Gold was not a priority.

But Yusuf didn't wait for her answer. He pulled a red velvet pouch out of his jacket pocket and placed it on the table, next to Warda's purse. "Look," he said. He loosened the string, revealing a thick, embellished gold bangle that he set on top of the pouch. "It's for you."

Warda immediately reached for the bangle. She eyed it carefully, taking in the details, the floral design wrought throughout. She stretched out her hand and lifted the bangle up and down as if it was on a scale. "It's heavy," she said. "Is it real?"

Yusuf laughed. "Of course it's real. Twenty-one karat. Put it on." He held her forearm and pushed the bangle to her wrist.

Warda couldn't help but admire it, turning her arm from side to side. The only gold she owned was a nameplate necklace she'd had since she was a little girl. She moved her wrist around a little longer, and then took the bangle off. "It's nice," she said.

"It's for you," he said again.

"I can't take it."

Yusuf looked alarmed. "What do you mean? I got it for you."

"Yusuf. I'm getting married."

"I got a job," he said.

She stared at him. "Good for you," she finally said.

"You think I can't do anything for you, but I can. He never brought you gold! I told you I wanted to marry you. I told you—", and then he began to cry.

Warda looked around, horrified. She pleaded with Yusuf to stop crying until he wiped his eyes with his jacket sleeve. He did not seem at all embarrassed. He started to tell her his plan. How he would save up for a wedding. How nobody would even remember that she had been engaged to Daud. Girls were getting divorced and remarried all the time— that was a lot worse than breaking off an engagement. To placate him, Warda nodded and said she would think about it. She told him she'd had no idea he cared so much for her. Inwardly, she regretted the meeting and vowed to never see him again. She pushed the bangle towards Yusuf.

"No, please!" He leaned closer and whispered, "It's my gift."

Warda smiled. He *was* trying to prove himself. She picked up the bangle again and held it with both hands. It was beautiful. She didn't have anything like it — anything so valuable. She placed the bangle back in the red velvet bag and pulled the string to tighten the opening.

"I will only take the bangle," she said, "if you keep it between us." She told him, partly to make him happy and partly because it was the truth, that out of all the gifts she had ever received, his was her absolute favourite. She would never forget it. Yusuf, grinning, took the velvet pouch out of her hands and dropped it into her purse.

In her bedroom, Warda pulled out a white shoebox on the bottom of the shelf, causing the one on top to fall into its place. She set the shoebox on her bed, listened at the door, and then closed it. Inside the box was the pair of white, sequined pumps she wore on her wedding day. Warda turned the left shoe upright, reached into the toecap, and pulled out the red velvet bag. The bangle slid out easily, and like always, she was dazzled by the glint of the gold. Warda slipped the bangle onto her right wrist and stretched it out before her. She looked at herself in the mirror. She had no choice but to steal little moments like this when she was at home alone because she could not risk wearing the bangle in public.

After she had changed her phone number and gotten married, Yusuf started passing messages to Warda through Filsun. At first, he demanded she give the bangle back. Warda stared at Filsun, doing her best to look both mystified and disturbed. She denied having any idea what he was talking about. Then Yusuf's story changed. He had not *bought* the gold. It was his sister's. He had taken it from the locked jewellery box she kept under her bed. His sister had learned that her bangle was missing and was going to report him to the police if he didn't return it to her by the end of the month.

Warda was shocked. She didn't know where Yusuf had gotten the gold bangle, but she hadn't imagined that he would steal it. Still, she figured she couldn't give it back. It was too late. And it was his fault. The more Warda thought about it, the more smug she became, because she understood that she had outwitted someone who had tried to manipulate her. Yusuf had tried to bribe her with gold — con her, even — thinking it would sway her, that it would cloud her judgement and make her go back on her decision to marry Daud.

He had underestimated her greed. Her vanity. Her desire to — even if no one else knew — possess something precious and expensive that belonged to her, and her alone.

∽

DAUD CAME HOME around five a.m. Warda was back in bed, pretending to be asleep. He threw open the bedroom door and turned on the light. Warda immediately sat up, pulling the covers. She had to wait for her eyes to adjust to the light before she could take in Daud's appearance. He was opening drawers and pulling out the contents, throwing clothes behind him and onto the bed, the floor. He looked haggard and frenzied but determined. His shoes were still on.

"Where is it?" he asked when he had emptied all the drawers. He moved to the wardrobe, going through jacket pockets. He pulled the shoeboxes off the shelf and threw them to the floor. "Where is it, Warda? Come on. Where is it?"

"Where is what? Are you crazy?" She stepped over the mess he had created, her eyes glimpsing the white, bedazzled pumps that had been flung across the room. She breathed a sigh of relief that she had answered Filsun's call and switched her hiding place. The red velvet pouch holding the gold bangle now rested safely in the middle of a three-kilogram bag of basmati rice, under the kitchen counter. Daud would never find it.

He snorted, and then gave her a look. "Where is the gold?"

"Gold?"

"Didn't that guy Yusuf give you some gold?"

"Yusuf," she said slowly, like someone attempting to make sense of the situation, "gave *me* gold?"

"That's what he says."

Cautiously—and she knew it was a risk—she let amusement show on her face. "I didn't know Yusuf had gold."

Daud held her gaze. "He doesn't have shit. He steals from his family. That's the kind of person he is."

For a second, shame washed over Warda. Was she that kind of person?

She shook her head and began rummaging through the clothes on the floor. She found the little clear case where she kept the gold nameplate she'd had since she was a child. She wore it for months at a time, and then got sick of it on her neck and put it away. She pulled it out and held it for Daud to see. "This is the only gold I have. And this—" She raised her left hand, where she was wearing a simple band on her ring finger.

He waved them away. "No. Not those. Do you have anything else? A bracelet?"

"No. I don't have *anything!*" Warda stood there, taken aback by the sadness in her own voice. It wasn't technically true, but somehow, it was how she always felt.

She placed her nameplate necklace on the dresser and walked out of the bedroom. Mechanically, she prepared her coffee in a moka pot and set it on the burner. She was thinking about what to do with the bangle. She could not keep it *now*, as beautiful as it was. She considered trading it at an Indian jeweller, but then she would have to explain how the new item had come into her possession. She could sell it and keep the money—though she had no need for money. She wanted gold. She wanted a jewellery case with a keypad lock like her aunt and Yusuf's sister had. She wanted something heavy with a handle that she could hide in her wardrobe and bring out whenever she was going to a wedding or a party. The sound of the bubbling coffee brought Warda back to her senses. She turned the burner off and set the moka pot aside.

She went to the bathroom, turned on the faucet, filled up the mini green watering can she used to wash herself, and used the toilet. She heard a knock on the bathroom door and Daud softly calling her name, but she ignored him. She washed her face with warm water and black African soap and moisturized with cocoa butter. Daud knocked again. Warda opened the door dramatically. She feigned anger and disappointment, though she was mostly uneasy. Despite what Filsun believed, they rarely fought.

"I'm sorry," he said.

Warda didn't look at him. She poured out a dime-sized drop of almond oil and worked it through her short, curly hair—the result of a bad texturizer at the salon that had made her hair break off. She had taken it surprisingly well.

Daud took a step closer to her, so that he was leaning

against the sink. His body was facing Warda, but she was still looking at herself in the mirror. "Forget about it. He's a liar. Maybe he thought I'd pay him off. It didn't work."

Warda played with a curl by her forehead, twisting it around her index finger. "I deserve gold," she said.

She would trade the bangle, she decided. She would get, in exchange, a set of thinner bangles — four or five, so that they moved and clinked on her wrist. And she would say, if anyone asked, that they were her aunt's, and that she was just borrowing the jewellery for an event, even though her aunt had never once, even after Warda's engagement, offered to let her wear any of her gold pieces. They hardly visited each other anymore anyway.

Daud watched Warda in the mirror. "You do," he agreed, and he gently kissed her on the cheek.

Welland, 2000

PRINCE CHARLES DRIVE was a cul-de-sac of thirty relatively new subsidized townhouses, one eight-storey apartment building, a playground, and two separate basketball nets (not courts). At the end of the drive was a small hill of grass that children tobogganed down in the winter, and beyond that, a back road, a pebbled expanse, and the Welland Canal. There were four other Somali families living in the co-op. When Jija Hussein went to look at an available unit with her cousin Mulki, she observed two women standing on a porch a few houses away. Mulki greeted them as soon as she got out of the car and the women gave shallow smiles and nods. One of them was a light-skinned woman wearing a plaid skirt, a knit sweater, and a sash wrapped around her head. She was holding her keys behind her back and had one foot on the first step of the porch, where the other woman stood, dressed in a baati, her dyed red hair tucked behind her ears. Mulki, who had never met the women before, introduced Jija to them and explained that Jija hoped to move into their neighbourhood. They made small talk while Jija looked around for the property manager. The woman holding the keys said her name was Sofia. The red-haired woman was Zainab. After a few minutes, Jija spotted the property manager walking over from the building where the office was located.

The unit was clean and spacious, with grey carpeting in all the main rooms and on the stairs. There was a powder room and a small backyard. There was an unfinished basement that could be used for storage. Most of all, there was light. The kitchen window bathed the whole space in sun. The large sliding back door revealed grass and weeds and, a little farther out, a sturdy, tall wood fence with the blue sky above it. Jija felt like she could begin again in this home. That staring out from these windows wouldn't be dangerous. She would not have to confine her children in such close quarters, always inside a nine-hundred-square-foot apartment. Instead, they could run outside and play; she could allow that.

She moved in the next month — June, not even waiting for the school year to end. She spoke to her children's teachers in advance, so that they could assign and collect any work or administer any tests required. But she quickly got the sense that it hardly mattered. They were only in elementary school. The teachers tilted their heads sympathetically and made general comments about how her kids would be missed.

Jija had the number of a Pakistani man with a truck who was starting a moving company. When the truck pulled out of her new driveway, and all her furniture was in the proper rooms, Jija had only to unpack the boxes and organize her things. She let her children go off to the park because they had been begging her all morning. Not even ten minutes later, Sofia and Zainab rang the doorbell. They were there to help her. Together, they assured her, they would get her settled in just a few hours. And they were right. They stayed close to Jija. Opening boxes. Emptying the contents. Asking where she wanted to put the glassware, the plates. Sofia was meticulous about wiping out all of the cabinets. And then they moved upstairs. Zainab organized the linen closet. Sofia and Jija quickly filled the bathroom cupboard, hung the shower curtain, and, after some searching for misplaced Zellers bags, laid a new bathmat in front of the sink.

Next were the children's rooms. Jija had three boys who would share one room and two girls who would share the other. The boys' room was slightly bigger, with a bunk bed and a single bed placed against opposing walls and a dresser between them. The women put away the boys' clothes and did the same in the girls' room, and by then,

Jija was exhausted. She was ready to thank the women and leave her room in its disorderly state, but Sofia and Zainab wouldn't hear of it. By the time the sun had begun to set, they had flattened the empty boxes and tied up the garbage bags and taken them out to the bins next to the building, calling all of their children home.

JIJA HUSSEIN HAD always imagined she would live an easy life — buoyed by family status, beauty, wealth, and a man who would, on her behalf, deal with any unpleasantness that arose. Instead, the man she chose made life more unpleasant for her, shirking all responsibility and leaving her to feed and change and bathe five children under eight. She had grown up with house girls and a driver and the promise of an education abroad, but all she got was refugee status and a teacher husband whose qualifications didn't translate and who no longer had the ambition to succeed anyway. They were in a new country. They had to do things differently. Did she think being a minister's daughter meant anything over here?

At first, Jija refused to admit that her station in life had changed. She and her husband settled in Toronto in 1992, moving to 320 Dixon Road with their infant daughter. She fell pregnant year after year and struggled to manage with such small children. She cooked and cleaned but took pains to ensure she didn't burn her forearms on the oven, cut herself, or have coarse, dry hands. She held her head high in public, especially when she came across other Somalis, and she didn't greet them if she didn't know them. Then one afternoon, on a brittle February day, as she was loading her groceries into the trunk of a cab and goading her kids to get in despite the protests of the driver, who realized too late that there wasn't enough space for them all, she slipped on a patch of ice and fell on her side. A middle-aged Somali couple who had exited the No Frills with their yellow grocery bags in hand were walking to their parked car and witnessed Jija's fall. The wife carefully placed her bags on the snow-covered ground and ran to help Jija up, while her husband shouted from afar, in a Northern accent, to ask if she was okay. Jija nodded vehemently, embarrassed, and thanked the older woman, quickly rushing into the cab and shutting the passenger door. In the shower that night, she looked at her sore hip, which was turning purple. Although the injury healed in a few weeks, Jija would feel, over time, as though she were constantly bruised on her side, forever nursing the hurt and humiliation that she was forced to endure.

Her children became resentments, shackles that only she was burdened with, while their father gallivanted around the city. Finally, she kicked him out. She was tired of him coming home in the early hours of the morning.

Tired of receiving phone calls from acquaintances who had heard that he was seen leaving a sketchy apartment in the 340 building, where losers were known to sit around all day chewing khat. Appalled, Jija pictured him with a disgusting wad bulging from his cheek, and no matter what she did, she couldn't get that image out of her mind. She threw his clothes into a suitcase, waited for him to come home, and tossed the suitcase right out the door when he did. He left, shaking his finger at her, warning her not to call him for help. Jija was unsettled by this parting remark—she was determined not to need anyone's help.

She snapped at her children for making messes and trained them to be self-sufficient: to fix their cereal and peanut butter and jelly sandwiches, to never turn on the stove or oven or answer the door, to sit quietly while they watched cartoons and not to disturb her in her bedroom. Her doctor prescribed her antidepressants, which mostly made her sleepy or indifferent. She bought a television set for her bedroom and only came out to use the bathroom, prepare dinner, and make sure the children went to bed after they had washed up. She developed a fear of being alone in the apartment and usually slept until the children were back from school because every time she was in the open kitchen by herself she felt the balcony subtly beckoning her. She lived on the eighteenth floor and had only been on the balcony when the landlord had shown her and her husband the apartment. She had reservations about renting the unit because it was so high; she was concerned about her daughter unlocking the balcony door and having a terrible accident. The landlord, who was the father of young children himself, agreed to install a chain lock up high, for her peace of mind. Since the day they moved in, the balcony had been off limits. But one weekday morning, Jija sent her kids off to school and couldn't return to sleep. She rose to make tea. While the water boiled, she watched the balcony door, with its gold handle and easy-to-reach chain lock. She unlocked the first door and had to use considerable force to pull it open, pushed past the screen door, and stepped towards the rusty railing. She took in deep breaths of air and looked out to the horizon: the looping roads and tiny cars, and then the other buildings, like blades of grass, shooting up in all directions. She leaned closer, using her body weight to rest, even more, against the railing. She heard it creak. She wondered, what if she fell? She looked down and imagined herself sprawled on the pavement, a pool of blood around her head. Disturbed by her own thoughts, Jija pushed off the railing and backed away.

She bought an old model Subaru from an elderly Yemini woman in the building who could no longer drive. That Saturday, she packed her children into the car and took the 403 west to St. Catharines. Jija looked good—she looked like herself. She had applied lipstick and powder, clipped her hair in the back, and sprayed her Anaïs Anaïs perfume. They were going to stay with Mulki, who had tried in vain to connect with Jija through phone calls and visits when she, too, had lived in Toronto, but Mulki eventually tired of Jija's cold shoulder and left her alone. Then Mulki left the city for the quiet suburban streets of St. Catharines. Jija had called Mulki after stumbling back inside from the balcony, rambling and apologetic, trying to explain in her ashamed, roundabout way why she couldn't bear to stay in her apartment any longer. Mulki understood.

There were plants in every corner of her two-bedroom apartment, and the sliding glass door to her balcony was always open during the warmer-than-usual spring weekend, letting in floods of light and fresh air. Mulki had two preteen daughters, Amira and Maryam, who gave up their room for Jija's boys. Mulki's girls slept on thick comforters they laid out on the living room carpet, and Mulki slept on the sofa, giving up her queen-size bed for Jija and her daughters.

Despite her orderly home, Mulki was unbelievably welcoming and tried to cater to Jija's children in a way that Jija seldom did. She handed them the remote control, ordered pizza, and then suggested they all go to the park downstairs after they had eaten. Jija followed reluctantly, sitting next to Mulki on a park bench, watching her children run and take turns on the swings. She knew that she had to move out of that building in Dixon if she wanted any kind of life. Jija turned to Mulki and asked her how she had found her co-op apartment.

JIJA, SOFIA, AND ZAINAB came to rely on each other in a way that, at first, made Jija uncomfortable but then, gradually, relieved. They watched each other's children if one of them had a doctor's appointment. They called each other up if one was going to the grocery store in case the others had run out of milk or bread or some other staple. Every month or so, after putting their kids on the school bus in the morning, they drove to Toronto to pick up a supply of halal meat, qahwah, spices, and sometimes halwa and biscuits. Sofia was always nervous on these trips, rushing the other women in front of the butcher's counter and repeatedly asking for the time. She worried that they would get stuck in traffic, or be held up by some other unforeseeable circumstance, and not make it back home by the time the children got off the bus. But she always worried needlessly. By two p.m., Jija's Subaru would make the left turn back onto Prince Charles Drive, and Sofia would be packing her ground beef, lamb meat, and chicken drumsticks into the freezer when her kids came through the door.

Sofia was like that, Jija learned. Delicate. Hyperaware of her surroundings, the expressions of others. Her home was impeccable. Her children—four daughters—barely did any chores. She assumed every responsibility, exhausting herself, and Jija pitied her for this. She wondered: *Why? For whom?* When Zainab once made a remark about them all being single mothers, Sofia had corrected her—she wasn't technically separated from her husband, only physically. He worked in Columbus, Ohio, and called her often, using international calling cards. At least twice a year, he sent a box full of clothing and shoes for the girls, all name brands: Nike Air Max shoes, Adidas T-shirts, and red Ohio State sweatshirts. Sofia had come to terms with the situation and stopped asking when he'd come back. She was a woman who had always worked; her mother had pulled her out of school when she was only thirteen to help in her stall in the market. Sofia's parents were divorced, so when her father remarried and his new wife died in childbirth, it was Sofia who was sent to Hamar to help raise her newborn twin brothers. She always went where she was needed and did what had to be done.

How different their lives had been. When the three of them spent time together that first year in Prince Charles Drive, Jija found herself slipping back into remembrances of her life in Somalia. Raised in a villa with a gate, where she had a large bedroom with an adjoining veranda, Jija only had to call out and someone would appear to meet her requests. Her father hosted lavish dinners with the freshest goat meat and influential guests: generals and ministers and journalists for the BBC Somali Service. She could tell that Sofia and Zainab liked hearing her stories — Zainab in particular, because she asked pointed questions and looked at Jija with the curious gaze of someone who accepts what they're told because they have no way of verifying it.

One evening, the women were sitting in Jija's living room, admiring the new three-piece sofa set that had just been delivered from the Brick. It was ivory with wide forest-green stripes. Zainab sat on the loveseat, spreading her hands against the smooth fabric. They began to talk about home. Sofia and Zainab, who were both from Beledweyne, were discussing a particular flood but couldn't agree on the year that it had happened. And then Jija mentioned Idi Amin's visit to Mogadishu in 1972 and the grand celebration of the revolution that her father had taken the whole family to watch. Gymnasts in short skirts performed, holding red flowered wreaths in a kind of ethereal fluid motion, while large slogans appeared behind them in English. Her father beamed. She had the impression, in that stadium, that she was living in the greatest country in Africa. The greatest country in the world. If she had ended her story there, it would have been fine. But Jija went on. There was something else she had to impart to Sofia and Zainab, something they might not have understood about her father. The fact that they could be in the stands, President Siad Barre and

Idi Amin seated just rows in front of them. The power. The prestige. Which Jija was sure—just by observing, by being close to—had been transmitted to her.

It was as if someone had subtly taken a photo of her while she was speaking passionately, and then quietly placed it before her so Jija could see herself and the other women listening on both sides of her. So she could see where she was now—where she had ended up: on welfare, in subsidized housing, sitting on a couch she had purchased on impulse and could not pay for in full, with women she would not have even crossed paths with in Somalia. Jija began to feel comical. She thought of her ex-husband, who sometimes stopped short of laughing at her, as if she was ridiculous and self-important but nevertheless engaging and, ultimately, harmless. She ended her sentence meekly, shrugging. She never spoke like that again.

THE FOLLOWING YEAR, Zainab upgraded her VHS player to a brand new DVD player. Then a friend in Toronto offered to send burned copies of wedding videos to her in the mail. As soon as the DVDs arrived, Zainab called Jija and Sofia and set tea on the stove. They couldn't contain their excitement, pointing out women they knew or had heard gossip about, commenting on their diraacs, their jewellery, their hair. Sometimes they re-watched the videos they liked most.

When they went to Toronto, they stopped at the videographer's store, where he sold copies of weddings he'd recorded, sometimes without the permission or knowledge of the couple who had hired him. This was where Zainab picked up what would become her favourite wedding video. Although it was a couple years old, she chose it because the man behind the counter told her that Hassan Adan Samatar had performed at the wedding. The DVD had scrawled on it in black marker:

Yasmin & Samir

Sunday, June 24, 2001

Toronto, Canada

During their first viewing, Zainab was all praise. The bride was young—in her early twenties—beautiful. She had dimples and wore an A-line dress that was both simple and sophisticated. The groom was tall and lean, with a handsome, angular face and soft curls that disappeared into a fade. Eventually, there was a shift to American music, and the couple slow-danced to K-Ci & Jojo's "All My Life," shyly glancing at each other, self-conscious in front of the cameraman yet emboldened by their new relationship.

But a few months later, when they sat in Zainab's living room, bored, and Sofia suggested watching the video for the third time, Zainab clicked her tongue. She put it on anyway. "She stole him from her friend!" she said dismissively, as she took her place on the sofa.

"What are you talking about?" Sofia asked.

"It's true. Jamila told me," Zainab said. "He was supposed to marry her friend. And then this happened." She gestured to the TV.

Jija gave her a serious look. "You can't steal a man."

"Who knows what happened?" Sofia interjected in a neutral but dismissive tone, wanting only to enjoy the video.

Zainab rolled her eyes. "I don't like it," she said.

Yet Jija noticed that Zainab couldn't help but watch. She couldn't help but stare at the young couple with wonder and aversion and, although she would never admit it, admiration. Jija smirked to herself and reached for one of the chocolate-filled wafer cookies Zainab had put on a plate. It seemed ridiculous to her: bickering about the supposed actions of a random young man in a wedding video when they barely spoke about the men they had married. A fleeting notion Jija once had returned—the feeling that each woman secretly pitied the other two, and that each woman believed that, no matter how bad her own circumstances, at least she had not been as naive or mistreated as the others.

For instance, Jija had been living on Prince Charles Drive for over three years when Zainab quietly reconciled with her ex-husband. Jija discovered this when she went to return Zainab's heavy glass casserole dish. She waited on Zainab's porch, shivering in her unzipped coat, rapping on the door while she held the dish against her ribs. Zainab finally answered, and Jija, her nose running, saw a tall, dark man who was the spitting image of Zainab's eldest son, standing at the end of the hall in an undershirt. Zainab seemed embarrassed, like Jija had caught her in a lie, or worse, a compromising situation. But Jija was quick-witted and courteous, greeting him with a raised hand while she backed away. By spring, he was gone again, and Zainab returned to her bustling, involved, wry self.

The three women were sitting at Zainab's kitchen table when she began to make distracted comments about the brief reunion—she must have felt she owed Jija and Sofia an explanation—about how she had tried, how her husband was a difficult person, and how her children couldn't blame her. Jija turned her head out of awkwardness and caught sight of Zainab's daughter, Rabiya, who was putting a cup in the sink. Rabiya's brow was furrowed, her lips pursed. She wore the confused expression of someone being implicated in something they had no part in.

ZAINAB ANNOUNCED SHE was moving to Ottawa at the annual co-op barbecue that summer. Her children were getting older and her son was doing poorly in high school. She complained about the calls she received when he skipped class, and although Jija made no mention of it, she had smelled the strong, earthy stench of marijuana on Zainab's son a few times. Zainab grumbled about the influence of white children and the lack of discipline from their lax parents who allowed them to drink alcohol and invite friends of the opposite sex over to their houses. She could no longer simply forbid her children, control what they were exposed to, even know *what* they were exposed to. And more recently, when she would show her disapproval at the behaviour of their friends, or even some kissing scene in a movie they were watching, they no longer hurried to explain or fast-forward. More and more, they had begun to stop anticipating — to stop being affected by — her reproach. But Ottawa was a bigger city. There was a bigger Muslim community. She hoped it wasn't too late for them to straighten out.

Jija understood. Her own children were growing up, and already, she could see muted intimations of what Zainab was contending with. But she had no intention of moving. Her children were better behaved. No matter how often she spoiled them — with fast food, swimming at the public pool, trips to Blockbuster to rent movies — there was a seed of distrust, a small fear that they allowed to recede most of the time but nevertheless remained alive in their memories.

Jija had no way of knowing that both she and Sofia

would be gone by the end of the year. That she would finally succumb to the importunate advances of a well-to-do, balding widower Mulki had introduced her to. That she would drive to Toronto to have lunch with him at Hamdi's. That she would agree to follow his Chevy Impala down Airport Road, and then a few turns more, until they were both parked in front of a five-bedroom house he had purchased in Brampton.

Or that Sofia would have the horrible luck of getting into a car accident on an icy back road. That she would stay in hospital for three weeks with a serious neck injury. That her husband, for the first time, would fly into Toronto from Columbus and drive a rental car down to Welland to take care of the girls. He visited her in hospital only once before it was time to take her home. Then he spoke animatedly about the insurance agents and lawyers who wanted to talk to her because they felt she was entitled to a payout from the city. After a few days, when Sofia had become accustomed to getting up and sitting down, and a physiotherapist had visited to massage her neck and help her with exercises, she told him he could go.

"Go where?" he said.

"Back to Ohio. Don't you have to work? I'm okay now."

"But what about the lawyers?"

They moved to Toronto, where he eventually squandered the insurance payout on bad business investments.

In the 2008 recession, he panicked and abandoned their three-bedroom condominium to foreclosure, to start over, alone, in Alberta.

Jija would surmise all of this from the bits and pieces she collected from Zainab when they spoke on the phone, which wasn't often. And just once, she ran into Sofia at the mosque after the Eid Al-Adha prayer, and they talked at length in the parking lot, holding each other's hands, asking after each other's children, feigning well-being.

Naturally, Jija, Sofia, and Zainab drifted apart without the glue of Prince Charles Drive to hold them together. They forgot how easily they had opened each other's doors, scolded each other's children, borrowed each other's things. Instead, if Jija heard one of their names, there was little more than an internal acknowledgement—*I know her.*

Toronto, 2005

SAMIR STOOD IN FRONT OF his apartment door—408—
and reached into his pocket for his phone. *NOKIA* flashed
across the screen, accompanied by the loud melody, which
startled him into holding the phone against his chest to
muffle the sound. He looked at the screen. *31 MISSED CALLS
from Yasmin.* He pushed the phone back into his jacket pocket
and hefted his keys in his left hand. His hands were always
coarse and dry and sore. He remembered when Yasmin
would look at him with alarm and pity because his skin
had cracked and run her long, smooth fingers between his.

He unlocked the door and walked in to the high-pitched
noises of a cartoon. He put his lunch bag down and slipped
out of his work shoes. When he stepped into the living
room, he saw Bilal lying on his stomach, facing the TV in
his Spider-Man pyjamas, his little hands holding up his face.

Bilal glanced at Samir, and then returned his attention to the cartoon.

"Where's your—" Samir heard heavy footsteps and turned his head. Yasmin appeared from the bedroom, holding the home phone loosely at her side. She was in a black lace bra and a heavily embroidered emerald-green gorgorad that stopped just above her navel. Her hair, which she had gotten done the day before, was free of its rolled pins and hairnet, falling in loose curls about her shoulders. "Oh."

Yasmin threw the phone. Samir ducked and heard it crash against the wall behind him. He looked back, his hands still instinctively protecting his head, and saw the phone parts scattered about the floor. He turned to Yasmin just in time to see her disappear into the bedroom and slam the door.

Samir stood there for a moment, and then picked up the phone parts. He looked at Bilal, whom he had briefly forgotten, and noticed that the child was sitting up and staring at him.

"It's okay," Samir said. He sat on the couch, directly behind Bilal, and put the battery back into the phone, snapping on the cover. He checked to see if it was working, and then placed the phone on the arm of the couch. Bilal was still staring at him. "Don't worry," Samir said. He reached for Bilal's shoulder, wanting to press it gently, but Bilal leaned away and turned back to the television.

Samir rubbed the back of his neck and stood up jerk-ily. He hesitated in front of the bedroom door and finally opened it. Yasmin was sitting at the vanity, drawing on her eyebrows. Her back was to him, bare except for the bra strap, which was too tight, causing her smooth brown flesh to bulge slightly. He watched her through the mirror.

"I'm going," she said. "And you're taking me. Since you made me miss my ride."

Samir leaned against the door frame. "I'm tired."

She turned to face him. "I don't care."

"What about Bilal?"

"We'll take him, too. Put him in the booster seat."

Samir exhaled.

"You always do this." Her voice almost broke. She was reaching into a polka-dotted cosmetics bag.

"I told you," he said. "There was an accident with one of the rental cars."

She turned to him again, using an eyeliner pencil to point to the alarm clock on the nightstand. "It's nine forty-three p.m."

"I had to fill out an accident report, and the guy couldn't —"

"I'm not stupid," she said, dropping her arm and glaring at him. It was true. He had never come home from work so late before. "You don't want me to go. Why don't you just say that?" She turned back to the mirror, stretched her left eyelid with her index finger and hastily swiped the eyeliner across her lid.

"I don't care," he said. "Go."

"I will."

Yasmin's green, glittery diraac was laid out on the left side of the unmade bed, where the comforter drooped awkwardly, almost touching the floor, and Samir's pillow was by the open closet, under a wet towel. He felt disrespected by the state of the room, and he felt the childish urge to pick up his pillow and carefully place it at the head of the bed but leave the rest of the mess the way it was. Or to push Yasmin's things onto the floor, too.

"You don't even know them," he said.

She rummaged in the makeup bag and pulled out two lipsticks.

"You don't even know them," he repeated, louder.

"I was invited."

He looked at her in the mirror, past her naked back. "Whore."

He watched her face for even the slightest tremor of indignation, but she just turned the lipstick cases upside down to read their names. He knew she wouldn't cry. He had lost — after the first year or two of marriage — the ability to make her cry. Instead, Yasmin tilted her head back and applied a deep-burgundy lipstick. Samir saw the whites of her eyes: how clear and determined they were.

~

WHEN SAMIR CAME OUT of the shower Bilal was watching *Caillou*. Yasmin was still in the bedroom, the door closed. He wondered why she wasn't ready. He half hoped that she had given up. That when he checked on her in a few minutes, he would find her asleep, clutching the comforter in her makeup and gold. The gold that he had gone to such trouble to get. He'd had to find a woman who was going to Dubai. He'd met with the woman — a short, round, middle-aged shopkeeper — at her stall in the market on Rexdale Boulevard. She'd had a constant grin on her face, huffing from behind the counter and in front of it, instructing a girl, presumably her daughter, to open boxes and lay out fabrics. He had found the little stall quite easily after asking for the woman by name. The other ladies, sitting behind cash registers that looked like plastic toys in their respective booths, merely pointed their fingers once they realized he was not there to buy from them. Or maybe their cold indifference stemmed from the unflattering rumours that were spreading about him.

But this woman didn't know who Samir was — he was sure of it. She said yes, she was going to Dubai. The box of stuff on the floor was from China, shipped to her by a contact. "Business, you know business?" She giggled, and then turned solemn. She didn't usually buy gold on behalf of customers because they complained about the styles she brought back and refused to pay. She preferred to pick up whatever jewellery she could and sell it to interested clients when she came home. It worked out better that way.

Samir told her he would pay up front and pulled an envelope out of his shirt pocket with two thousand dollars inside. He opened it slightly to show her the bills. Her eyes widened, and she took the envelope. She told him she was leaving the day after tomorrow, and it was a good thing he came when he did. He wanted a set? He showed her some pictures he had printed off the internet and had folded up in his other pocket. She glanced at the photos and told him it would be difficult to find the exact same designs, but she would try her best to find something similar. Samir nodded and wrote down his information on the back of a card she provided.

"For your wife?" The woman was grinning and bending her round face forward.

Samir said yes, though it wasn't true. They were not married yet.

He felt the sudden desire to confide in the woman. He looked at her lanky preteen daughter, who was laying out fabrics on top of one another according to whatever arbitrary system her mother had devised. He felt like confessing to the shopkeeper that he had actually left his fiancée for Yasmin — the girl he was buying the gold for. That his fiancée and Yasmin were once friends, that he had only met Yasmin because his fiancée had pushed her to join them at their table when she entered the restaurant they were dining in. He wanted to explain, just once, to some- one who might understand. He had already put a down payment on the banquet hall. He had sat in his fiancée's living room and had tea with her father and uncles. He had made promises he honestly intended to keep. He wanted to say that nobody sacrificed all of those things — money but, more importantly, their reputation — for no reason. And it wasn't because Yasmin was more beautiful. It was mostly because Yasmin didn't care. She was reckless in a way that he had never experienced before, and that inspired him to be reckless, too. Then all they had was each other, and that was enough.

Of course Samir didn't say any of this. He just left the market with his head down, his hard-earned money tucked into the folds of a stranger's handbag.

SAMIR HAD TO break off his engagement. To confirm what his fiancée had begun to suspect. He was a coward — he hid from her family. And they seemed too embarrassed to search him out and rebuke him. He decided to get it over with quickly, calling Rowda to come down from her apartment and telling her in his car while the engine ran.

He apologized profusely and made a show of looking at the time, since he had planned it so he would have no more than a ten-minute window until he had to set off for work. Once that part was over, he had only to deal with his friends and family, who, aside from being mildly amused, did not seem very invested either way.

In fact, he suspected that those in his circle who knew both Rowda and Yasmin understood him perfectly. Rowda was a year younger than Yasmin and attractive in her own right. She had an angular face and very long, thick lips that spread out above her chin. She was tall and fleshy, with a sonorous voice, but she was innately, almost proudly, vapid. Rowda was the kind of girl—and "girl," Samir realized, was the right word—who laughed and stared, wide-eyed, as a response. She fell to the background in almost every social situation, yet she was bizarrely intent on *being* social. She would arrange casual lunches and dinners at local restaurants, force Samir to come, and then sit back, quietly nibbling on a chicken leg while conversation buzzed around her. She wanted, he noticed, to always be at the centre of the action, but she did not possess the charm, or the resoluteness, or the capacity to be the action herself. Even her most unappealing friends would seem uniquely lively next to her. And she relished this. Like their outrageous stories and hilarious tangents were in some way a reflection of her.

Yasmin, however, was smaller, with a round face, dimples, and a slither of a gap between her two front teeth. She was neither thin nor shapely, yet there was something unmistakably feminine about her. She possessed an abrasive, even distasteful quality. She teased people mercilessly, wringing a joke dry in her hands long after anyone else found it humorous. Perhaps it was for this reason that Rowda and the rest of her friends held Yasmin at a distance. Their group dynamic seemed both dependent on her and fractured because of her. It was confusing to Samir, but he soon pinned it down to Yasmin's middling attachment to *them*—she was separate, whole, unfettered. Once, he witnessed her join the group at Tandoori Time, sit down, receive a call five minutes later, and leave abruptly after blowing air kisses. Rowda's friends mumbled about how rude Yasmin was and why she had even bothered to come if she had other plans. They threw out guesses as to where she might be going and who she might be meeting. They discussed, at length, the character of a divorcee named Raqiya that Yasmin had recently befriended. Samir was entertained by their conversation, though he disagreed with the conclusions they drew. He wanted to laugh at their ignorance. Yasmin was probably meeting a man, he thought. That idea, for whatever absurd reason, grew in his mind as he sat at that table, and made him incrementally more and more jealous.

~

THE VIOLET JEWELLERY CASE was open in Yasmin's lap, and her mother was leaning into her to get a glimpse when Samir expressed his hope that their wedding be quiet and hurried. They had not yet discussed details, only their urgent wish to get married.

Yasmin shot him a look that revealed pity but then scorn for that pity, which served as a rapid retraction. "But why?" She held up the gold necklace by both ends to her mother, who took it from her and examined it. "No, put it on me," she said in Somali, turning on the sofa so her back was to her mother.

"The thing is — because —" He was embarrassed that Yasmin was forcing him to articulate in front of her mother what she knew very well. "How everything happened," he finished limply.

Her mother hooked the necklace and said, "Let me see." She admired it on Yasmin's long neck.

Yasmin touched it with her fingers and smiled — whether at the necklace, her mother's praise, or Samir, he didn't know. She got up to look at her reflection through the glass doors and the mirrored backing of a china cabinet. After a long pause, she said, "Look at yourself! You're acting like a criminal. Why do we have to hide? That'll only make things look worse. Right, Hooya?"

Her mother spoke up then. She tried to make Samir see, with the force of her authority and the manipulative gentleness of a mother figure, that a big wedding was absolutely compulsory. Yasmin would not be given away without one. What did he expect? To plan an elaborate wedding for the other girl—both Yasmin and her mother managed to avoid saying Rowda's name—and then rush to marry Yasmin in a simple religious ceremony? As if it were a shotgun wedding? As if Yasmin were desperate and had not been raised with love and every luxury her parents could afford for the past twenty-three years?

"No!" she said, with an abrupt shake of her head and a snort that Samir found derisive but convincing.

So they'd had a wedding. One that ballooned into an event so ostentatious, Hassan Adan Samatar had agreed to sing a few songs. Mutual friends who had taken Rowda's side, and even called Yasmin to confront her, were spotted huddled in a group at a table near the exit. They congratulated Yasmin, taking photos with her or making a show of dancing with her in front of the camera. Any allegiance, any disdain, any distrust they held, seemed not to have necessarily faded away but rather to have been put away somewhere, so that it could be accessed at a more convenient time.

~

YASMIN EMERGED FROM the bedroom, the delicate green and gold fabric of her diraac trailing behind her. Both Samir and Bilal pretended not to notice. She had covered the top of her head with a sheer, shimmering gabasar, but a few curls framed her face. She pulled a pair of stilettos from the hall closet and sat in the armchair to put them on.

If Samir was honest with himself, he had expected more out of marriage. Above all, he had expected a certain gratitude on Yasmin's part that never manifested. Once they were actually married, the excitement and perseverance that had led them to that point had rapidly dissipated, and they were thrown headfirst into the drudgery of settling in, and then the grind of daily life.

There was also the matter of Yasmin's other ties—her mother and siblings and cousins and friends, including the divorcee, whom Samir disliked—which he felt he had to tear her from. She could only rest her eyes on him for a few moments before she was distracted again, and the distraction proved more insulting to him than the attention was gratifying, so he sulked. They moved to the west side of the city, practically Mississauga, which discouraged most visitors. When Raqiya or Yasmin's cousins came over, Samir, feeling self-conscious and uneasy in their presence, would pretend to be tired from work, and they would take the hint and rise to leave while Yasmin protested not to worry about him.

He wanted to get her pregnant right away, because he believed this would draw her closer to him, but she suffered little morning sickness and her entertaining was hardly impeded. It was the same when Bilal came — in fact, it was worse. Her entire family descended upon their cramped two-bedroom apartment. Her mother, sister, and cousins alternated their overnight stays for weeks. They minded the baby, mixing his formula and swaddling him expertly, cooking in huge batches, distributing the food into plastic containers and then storing them in the fridge. They took porridge and soup to Yasmin on a tray, and then helped her bathe. When they finally left, there was a quiet emptiness in the air. Yasmin had recovered but still spent most of the day in bed. Bilal, who had been passed from one person to the next in the earliest part of his life, hardly fussed, even when Yasmin just laid him on his back or left him in the bassinet.

When Bilal turned one, Samir would come home some Friday evenings to find the toddler standing by the door in a puffer coat with a yellow scarf wrapped around his neck, his diaper bag beside him. Yasmin would be running around the apartment, her coat hooked over her arm, looking for the Palmer's body lotion or children's Advil and directing Samir to take her to her mother's place. The first time, he obliged. But he hadn't realized that Yasmin and Bilal would be away the whole weekend, and that he would have to wait until Sunday night to be summoned to collect them. He started to make excuses. He'd just gotten off work. He was sleepy. He had not sat in traffic for over an hour just to get back on the road. Yasmin, who couldn't drive, would just stare pensively at the carpeted floor. But on a May afternoon, she called the divorcee while Samir was in the shower, and forty minutes later, Raqiya was in the entryway, holding Bilal on her hip while Yasmin carried the bags and instructed Bilal to wave goodbye to his father.

By that summer, those weekend visits to her family stopped and the random dinners with friends at Salaama Hut became few and far between. Samir never outright outlawed anything. Instead, he made things difficult for Yasmin, even impossible. He denied her money or hid her wallet. He put his hand to Bilal's forehead and expressed fear of a fever. He commented on her friends' reputations — what did that say about her? He complained about her cooking — when was the last time she had made something edible? Why couldn't she focus on being a good wife and mother instead of running around the streets of Toronto?

These words first escaped Samir in a heated moment of frustration. He banged his fist against the wall, his pointed remarks evolving into a full-blown tirade. He was able to focus on Yasmin — to really look at her — and he realized that she was unnerved. She struggled to keep her composure and then burst into tears. Her quick mouth, which often teased and retorted effortlessly in regular conversation, floundered. He had this, Samir thought, if nothing else. He had this power over her. And he began to use it often, following her to the kitchen or bedroom while he rambled. He framed his attacks as casual discussions, often beginning with "Can I ask you something?" before berating her with the self-possession of someone who was relaying simple observations. Someone who just wanted to know.

When Samir found his work shirt still in the pile of dirty laundry one morning, he held the shirt in front of Yasmin and criticized her, as she stood over the stove, making Bilal a pancake. He could see her breathing deeply as she gripped the spatula, but he did not anticipate her throwing the spatula at him, the handle hitting him directly between the eyes with an impact that rendered him speechless.

"What do you want from me?!" she screamed, panting like someone who was prepared to fight, despite looking terrified.

Her reaction startled Samir more than the throbbing in his head. It occurred to Samir that he could not name, exactly, what he wanted from Yasmin—only that he was painfully aware of feeling deprived, slighted, and underappreciated.

~

YASMIN'S OBSESSION WITH weddings began soon after.
It started with her younger cousin's wedding, which she
had to attend. And then the divorcee remarried and threw
a women's-only party, and Yasmin came home so elated
and luminous, Samir thought it might've done her some
good. But there was always another wedding. The daughter
of a family friend. A former neighbour's son. Her sister's
old classmate. Yasmin's connections to the people getting
married became increasingly tangential. Yet her efforts
grew. She begged Samir to watch Bilal, called the hair-
dresser in advance, and still had to wait hours to get her hair
done the day before a wedding. "The whole city is going to
this wedding! All of Toronto is going to this wedding!" she
would say to explain her tardiness when she came home
from the salon, sometimes just before midnight, with her
hair curled and pinned. He noticed that Yasmin's diraac
collection was growing, but Samir couldn't understand how
she was paying for them all.

One night, while Samir lay in bed, she held up two
metres of thin sky-blue material with a white swirl
design embroidered finely across it. "From France," she
announced. She let it fall over her head and threw one end
over her shoulder theatrically, her face beaming.

"Where did you get it?" Samir asked, his tone aggressive.

Yasmin stared at him. "From Ubah's store. On Weston Road."

"How much was it?"

She laughed. "Free."

But by free she meant that she could pay it off over the next year because Ubah had written Yasmin's name down in her spiral notebook, with three hundred dollars and her phone number.

Samir decided to try a different strategy. He would let Yasmin do what she wanted. He had to admit, she wasn't neglecting any of her duties. She still cooked dinner, bathed Bilal, and put him to bed before she readied herself and clicked off to the downstairs lobby, where she awaited a ride. She would grow tired of the weddings. She would get bored.

But Yasmin became even more dedicated. More enthusiastic. She counted down days in anticipation and relayed rumours over the phone about who might be singing at a particular wedding, whose parents had paid for the whole thing, and how the bride had dropped forty pounds in three months.

So he started arguments with her again. He rebuked her. He called her names. Yasmin learned to scoff and leave anyway.

Samir ran out of patience. One night, he stood before their front door, barring her way. He crossed his arms, his legs spread apart. "You're not going," he said matter-of-factly.

Yasmin was wearing a red guntiino, her right shoulder and arm bare and her waist cinched with the skilfully wrapped and tied fabric. Her hair was straightened and parted down the middle, and she was wearing drop earrings that shimmered and drew his gaze to her face. She looked glamorous, but her eyes couldn't hide her disgust. "Get out of my way. My ride's downstairs," she said, no strength in her voice.

Samir didn't move. "What are you doing?" he said, trying to match the combination of revulsion and resentment he knew she felt for him. "You're a married woman. You're a mother. Dressed like that? Honestly, Yasmin, have you ever asked yourself? What are you doing?"

She just gazed at him intensely, like she was bored and ready for his speech to be over.

"I'm serious. You're obsessed with these weddings! And for what? What are you getting out of it? Have you ever asked yourself? What you're—"

Yasmin took a step towards him, inching her face closer to his so that he could feel her small, rounded chest pressed against his folded arms. "I'm getting away from you!" she shrieked, her spittle hitting him in the face.

His ears ringing, Samir slapped her with a force he instantly regretted. He was flustered and alarmed by his own actions, but he tried his best to keep his expression neutral and stay put, watching like a guard as Yasmin caught herself from stumbling and reflexively held her cheek.

Samir heard a neighbour's door open. He turned and looked through the peephole. The middle-aged Polish woman who lived directly across from them had poked her head out of her door.

"Now move, or I'll scream," Yasmin said, her voice low and trembling.

Samir pressed his forehead against the door. He had no choice but to get out of her way.

NOW YASMIN STOOD before Samir, the heavy, musky scent of her oud perfume permeating the air. She was wearing the gold set he had bought her. Yasmin kept the gold locked in her jewellery case and hidden in the back of their bedroom closet, and she only brought it out to wear to weddings.

"Come on, Bilal. Let's go." She reached over the arm of the couch and grabbed the boy's sweater. Her heels clacking against the linoleum, she approached her son, put the sweater over his head, and eased his arms through. She combed the knotted back of his hair with her fingers and helped him into his shoes.

The three of them left the apartment and walked to the elevator in silence, Yasmin leading the way. Her shoulders were straight and she walked at a slow, fluid pace.

She pulled her cellphone out of her clutch and looked at the time while they waited for the elevator. Samir secured Bilal in his booster seat, got in the car, and asked Yasmin for the address. She looked in her clutch again and pulled out a piece of paper.

"3342 Castlegate Road," she read, and then handed him the paper. She told him the major intersection.

"Castlegate Road," Samir repeated, as he backed out of the parking space.

The ride was quiet except for the call Yasmin made to let Raqiya know she was on her way. She apologized, laughed loudly, and then hung up.

When they arrived at the banquet hall, guests were loitering out front. Men in suits smoked by the stairs, and women in brightly coloured diraacs walked across the parking lot. Whenever the doors opened they could hear the music, booming but indistinguishable.

"Okay. I'm going to come back with Raqiya. I have my keys. Put Bilal right to bed, but make him use the washroom first." Yasmin opened the door and stepped out.

A car honked somewhere behind him, but Samir kept his eyes on the rear-view mirror. He watched Yasmin move farther and farther away until she was out of sight and he had to turn his head to follow her. She was near the entrance, holding her diraac up with one hand as she climbed the steps. Samir's attention turned to a clean-shaven man in a grey suit standing by the landing. The man dropped his cigarette and put it out with his shoe, all while gazing at Samir's wife. Yasmin swung open the glass door and disappeared into the crowd.

Amsterdam, 2008

I WAS RELIEVED when Hooya started to visit Rashid Barre, even though she dragged me along with her. It was our first summer alone. I was ten. My father had died that fall after complications during his bypass surgery. My older brother, who for years had pestered Hooya for details about his own father, managed to learn enough from our uncle Ali, who came over from London for the funeral. Upti Ali couldn't stay sober and staggered to our house in the middle of the night, falling asleep on our doorstep when Hooya refused to let him in. Faisal was sixteen. His father was surprised to learn he *had* a son. After a few tense phone conversations with Hooya, he arranged a visit, and two weeks later, a stocky, middle-aged Italian man was sitting in our living room, stroking the back of Faisal's head like he was a cat. Hooya leaned against the arched entryway with her arms crossed, cordial but curt with her ex-husband. She had the air of someone who has done everything in their power to achieve a certain outcome, and finally, when they realize it's impossible, washes their hands of it all. Raffael tried to reminisce with her about their days in Rome, but she maintained a tepid disinterest. His aunt Nina had died some years "after Ladan ran away," as he put it. He told Faisal about his own family; he had remarried and had three daughters, all of whom were excited to meet their new brother. He pulled out his phone to show Faisal pictures. He promised to send for Faisal in the summer and take him to some beach town where they would lie on the sand and eat gelato. By the first of July, Faisal was packed and stuffing his suitcase into the boot of a taxi.

It seems strange to admit this — and I didn't truly grasp it until that summer when we were finally alone — but my mother made me uncomfortable. There were little things. Like when she would pull off my glasses and tell me to look at her, even though I couldn't see her clearly without them. Or when she would slap my hand when I picked unconsciously at my lips. But there was something else. Twice, she found me crying in bed. Both times, she appeared in the doorway, pushing it open with her slender fingers, and said, "What are you crying for?" I could tell she thought I was silly and dramatic because my father had been dead for months by then. "The Dutch girl is crying," she said to herself as she went down the stairs. She called me the Dutch girl because I was born in the Netherlands and sometimes corrected her grammar; Faisal was born in England, but she never called him the English boy.

I don't know how, or even when exactly, Hooya started working as a translator. She never talked about her job, and she didn't work while my father was alive. She only studied then, attending language classes here and there. As far as I knew, we didn't have a pressing need for money. After we buried my father, Hooya made an effort to sit with those who came to pay their respects. By the third or fourth day of the tacsi, I saw a familiar man pull Hooya aside. I spent days trying to place the man—tall but frail looking, with a henna-dyed goatee. I had absolutely seen him before. And then one day, when we were heading out to do the grocery shopping, Hooya stopped by Dahabshiil. I assumed she was sending money back home. I followed her inside, and there was the man, sitting at a counter behind the glass dividers; I recognized him from going to the Dahabshiil before with my father. I learned that my father had been investing money at the hawala over the years, and that he had about fifteen thousand euros sitting there, which went to my mother. She withdrew a few thousand and left the rest.

Hooya began her job the spring after my father's death. Some mornings, while Faisal and I readied ourselves for school, she would also be getting dressed to head out of the house. Faisal watched her with suspicion. Her hours were irregular, and we could never be sure if she would be there when we came home.

One afternoon, Faisal and I were in the living room, me reading on the sofa and him playing games on the computer in the corner.

"I'm hungry," I said. It was past five and Hooya still wasn't home.

Faisal took off his headphones and offered to make me a sandwich. I shook my head.

"Do you —" he faltered, "really believe she's working?"

I closed my book, holding my place with my index finger.

He cracked a smile, then turned back to the computer screen. "Maybe she'll run away again."

My mind went completely blank at those words, and I felt an irrational impulse to lunge at my brother. To scratch his face and pull his hair and tell him that his stupid father was a liar. But I just opened my book again, propping it up against my raised knees, and said nothing.

Since Faisal wasn't around to babysit me that summer, Hooya took me down the street to our neighbour's house. Although Hooya was only gone for a few hours three or four days a week, every single time, I would sit by the window so I could watch the street and pick at my lips. Every time, a quiet voice in my head would whisper that Hooya would not return. She had finally garnered enough willpower, and she had enough money, to start over in Oslo or Berlin or wherever. Faisal was with his father, and she had deliberately left me with the kindest woman in our neighbourhood, a big-boned, smiling habaryar, who had a gold tooth and indulged her children with so much food that they threw their weight onto other kids as torture.

But, eventually, I would see our silver Volkswagen Polo enter our street and park in front of our house. And then Hooya would walk towards me, her face betraying no secret thoughts. She would thank Habaryar and chat with her for a few minutes, and then we would go home, where she would ask me if I was hungry and, no matter how I answered, start cooking.

THEN SHE MET Rashid Barre. He was getting his annual physical and Hooya had been on standby as a translator for a few refugees and immigrants at the doctor's office. After the appointment, instead of walking to her car and leaving, she paid special attention to the elderly man who was heading to the bus stop. Hooya offered him a ride, which he reluctantly accepted. It turned out that he lived alone, on the bottom floor of a duplex nearby. When she took him home, Hooya followed him inside, even though he insisted he was fine. Thick layers of dust had collected on the TV stand, stacks of flyers were piled in the corners of the room, the floors needed a wash, and the curtains could use replacing. "We have to help him," she told me.

A few days later, Hooya brought a caddy of cleaning supplies and parked in front of Rashid Barre's house. I could see him push back a curtain at the window and stare out at us. Despite this, we had to knock on the door for at least two minutes before he answered, blocking our entry with his big body. Hooya slipped past him like he should've been expecting her. I stood awkwardly at the door as Rashid Barre looked back at her, annoyed. To me, he seemed large, though he was shorter than Hooya. He had a broad face, blubbery lips that always appeared wet, and a medium-brown complexion with a smattering of tiny dark moles framing his temples around his eyes.

Hooya told us to go sit in the kitchen or take a walk and immediately set to work in the living room. She tossed the stacks of flyers without asking. The old man grumbled his protestations meekly — Hooya didn't have to do anything, he was fine, he was going to get to it that week. But he sat down at his small kitchen table anyway, only getting up to open the back door as the strong scent of chemicals permeated the air and to fetch his Quran. I tried to stay close to Hooya, asking if I could help, but she shooed me away. She was busy wiping down surfaces and holding up the microfibre cloths so she could marvel at the amount of dirt she had collected. I wandered out the back door, where there was a small plot of overgrown grass and weeds, a clothesline with only pins on it, and a deflated basketball. I sat on the flattened ball and picked my lips.

Over an hour later, Hooya called to us both. She had parted the curtains and opened the front window, and the sun's brightness reflected off the shiny wood floors and the dark television screen. Somehow she had managed to find clean bedding for the daybed that lined the window and carefully placed fluffed pillows upright. There was no more clutter. She opened the cupboards of the TV stand to show us how she had organized the bulky electronics and various Islamic books, leaving out only the remote control. Rashid Barre just grunted an acknowledgement and went to sit on the daybed.

Hooya didn't seem to care. She reached for the dirty bedsheets that were crumpled on the floor. "I'm just going to wash these," she said, walking to the kitchen where the washing machine was.

She returned ten minutes later with three cups of tea balanced on a dinner plate. Since the old man didn't have a coffee table she set it on the rug in front of him. She carefully handed him a cup, gave me one that was extra milky, and then sat down with her own.

"Don't you have any children?" Hooya asked.

Rashid Barre was sipping at his tea cautiously. "Of course I have children."

"Where are they? In Rotterdam?"

"America."

"America?"

"Two of them. One is in South Africa. The other three are in Somalia."

Hooya's legs were crossed, and she was holding the bottom of her cup with her left hand. "Do you have other relatives nearby? Maybe nieces or nephews. Cousins?"

He shook his head.

"So you're really alone?"

He didn't respond, and in that moment, I realized that Hooya made Rashid Barre uncomfortable, too.

"I don't understand. Why didn't you go to America to be with your children?" she continued, unbothered by his silence.

"It didn't work out that way," he said, his tone irritated and final.

I guess Hooya knew to stop pressing. She gulped down her tea, while I had only taken a few sips. "Hurry up," she said, nudging me gently with her elbow.

In the car, she was pensive. "See, he has six children and he's still alone!" She looked at me for a while, as though to ascertain whether I understood the gravity of this. "Haven't you noticed," she added, "that Faisal hasn't called us once?"

I was sitting in the passenger seat, trying to formulate an appropriate response, but I was suddenly flustered by how beautiful my mother looked. Her long neck was turned to me, and her face appeared so soft, her cheekbones so sharp, her teeth perfectly square behind her full, parted lips. But it was a passing thought that I refused to dwell on because admitting her beauty, even to myself, gave Hooya some credit that I preferred to deny her. My mother, who had grown used to my reticence, started the car and drove off.

HOOYA FORCED ME to call Rashid Barre "Awoowe," despite the fact that she'd been telling me for years that all of my grandparents were dead. As our visits became more frequent, I realized that his grumpiness was an act—a mask that attempted to hide any recognition of the ease my mother was bringing to his life. After a couple weeks, she had brought his two-bedroom apartment up to her standards. She went through his cupboards, throwing away any canned goods that were expired. She cleaned out his refrigerator. She bent down on her haunches and scrubbed the tiles of his bathroom. She washed the walls. She threw out his curtains and hung up a pair of cream, floral panels she had purchased on sale at IKEA. One afternoon, all three of us drove up the main road to the Dirk van den Broek, where Hooya methodically picked out staple foods and, as if he were a child, encouraged Awoowe Rashid to get what he wanted. At the cash register, she moved to the end of the conveyor belt and started bagging the groceries. Awoowe Rashid just stood there in his suit jacket, in spite of the hot weather.

"It's your food," my mother finally said, after the cashier had called out the price and looked back and forth between them.

The old man reluctantly reached for his wallet and paid by card. He grumbled all the way home about how Hooya had purchased the whole store, including things he didn't need. At his place, I helped Hooya put the food away. She was smiling the whole time, like she had achieved some obscure victory.

"Trust me, he needs all this," she said. "It's no good to be cheap about food."

She gave me a yogurt cup and cut up some peaches on a plate for Awoowe Rashid. She had an appointment interpreting for a man who was seeing a family lawyer and would be back to cook dinner. When she returned, she made rice and salmon, with roasted potatoes and herbed green beans. We never used the kitchen table, at least not together. Instead, we sat in our respective corners of the small living room with our plates perched on our knees and glasses of juice at our feet. Awoowe Rashid ate quietly with his hands, his head lowered over the plate. When he finished, he looked up at Hooya, a grain of rice stuck just under the fold of his lower lip.

"Give me a little more," he said, holding out his plate.

Usually, these visits ended with Hooya questioning Awoowe Rashid. She was embarrassingly inquisitive about the old man's children—especially his daughters in America. If the question was straightforward enough, Awoowe Rashid would answer. Then Hooya would inch closer to the heart of her curiosity—why had they abandoned him? She never said it so plainly, but I knew she was always skirting this question.

One of his daughter's, the younger of the two, had visited him twice. She had last been in the Netherlands three years before and stayed for as long as she could without a visa: three months. She had young children, the youngest of whom she had brought with her. Now they were all in school, and her truck driver husband was often away from home for days at a time. Yet Awoowe Rashid revealed little about his older daughter; he wouldn't even tell Hooya her name. Sometimes he snapped and asked what any of it had to do with her, and she would admit, undaunted, that it had nothing to do with her at all. That was the point at which she usually told me to pack up my little bag with my colouring things or my book. We would leave while an impotent but steady tension remained in the air, until the next time we visited, when it would have seemingly evaporated.

Then, in mid-August, Awoowe Rashid pre-empted the questioning and asked Hooya when she had come to the Netherlands.

"Eleven years ago. Maybe twelve? Yes, it was ninety-six."

"How?"

"I was in England. Living with my brother and his family. I had my son, too. You haven't met my son. He's sixteen. And then I met her father." She nodded towards me. "He was visiting friends in London, but he was a Dutch citizen, so ... we married and I came here. That's how."

Awoowe Rashid had a quizzical look on his face, like, somehow, she had evaded his question. "How did you get to London?"

I snuck a glance at Hooya. Her eyebrows were raised. I knew that look; she was wary. "That's a long story." An odd current existed between them—almost a standoff. It was as if each of them was assessing whether to give up or to push even more, to arrive at something even remotely meaningful. Hooya must have wondered what Awoowe Rashid might have heard about her first marriage, but I got the sense that he was not deeply interested in her the same way she was in him. His questioning was retaliatory. Perhaps he did it to show her how unsettling such prodding was. Regardless, Hooya didn't hesitate for long. She treated the rest of that interaction like a hoop she had to jump through: "I was living in Rome. Working there. I met a man—Faisal's fath—"

"When did you get to Rome?"

"1990, I think. The winter of 1990."

"And how? You were how old?"

"I was eighteen."

"Where were you from again?"

"Hamar," she said.

"So you left Hamar at eighteen?"

"Yes."

"How?"

Hooya laughed lightly. "With a visa. That was the only way."

"How did you get a visa?"

"Through my father. He had a friend at the embassy. He made his friend promise to arrange our visas before he was arrested. He left us with some cash, and it was just enough. You had to pay for the visa and show you had enough money to support yourself for a while."

The old man sat sullenly on his daybed.

"My brother and I left together. It was just in time, really. Things got pretty bad after that. You've been here for almost ten years, right?" Hooya asked, returning the focus to Awoowe Rashid.

"Yes, but I'm not a citizen," he spat, his voice raised. "I'm still a refugee!"

Hooya looked taken aback. I think Awoowe Rashid felt bad, because he added, his voice slightly lowered, "Maybe next year. Maybe they'll give me citizenship next year."

~

I WAS ALMOST as surprised as Hooya when Awoowe Rashid passed her his cordless phone. He didn't often get calls when we were there, but if he did, he held the phone pressed to his ear, rushed into his bedroom, and closed the door. I was sitting on the floor between Hooya's legs, while she untied one of the braids that was starting to come undone at the back of my head.

"Hello? Yes? Oh, yes . . . Yes, nice to meet you, too, Firdowsa."

I could easily hear the loud, raspy voice of the woman on the other end. She began to ramble energetically. She thanked Hooya for all of the ways she had been helping her father in the past few weeks. She remarked that it was a blessing they had met. That he was grumpy and difficult, but really, he practically bragged about Hooya.

"We live so close by, it's really no problem . . . Ameen, ameen. Thank you. Are you the older one? Oh? And where do you live again? . . . Yes, but where exactly? . . . Oh, Minnesota. How is it there?"

I wondered anxiously if Hooya would turn her usual interrogation on Awoowe Rashid's daughter. Awoowe Rashid was in the bathroom doing his ablutions for Asr prayer—this was her chance. But Hooya was polite the whole time. After a few more minutes of conversation, they hung up and Hooya redid my braid.

When Awoowe Rashid finished praying, he folded up his

prayer mat and hung it across the iron foot of the daybed. He sat and recited dhikr, ticking his remembrances off on each joint of his right hand with his thumb and index finger. Hooya mumbled about boiling water for pasta and went to the kitchen, but she quickly returned.

"Upti Rashid, what a mess you made! There's water everywhere."

Awoowe Rashid looked confused. "In the bathroom?" he asked. "But it's always like that. I have to use the shower head for wudu." He looked at me when he said this, as if I might understand and explain it to my mother on his behalf.

"No, in the hall!" she said. "Come look. Come."

We both got up to look. There was a small pool of water in the hall, just outside the bathroom door. Hooya reached into the washing machine and pulled out a dirty pillowcase to dry the floor. She waved us away, irritated, and put a big pot of water on the stove. She sat at the kitchen table to wait. Then we heard, "Allah!"

I looked into the hall, where a tiny pool of water had begun to form again, the size of a two-euro coin. Hooya craned her neck to find both an expansive brown water stain and a slightly sagging ceiling. "It's leaking," she said with a sigh.

She called the emergency maintenance number on the magnet stuck to the fridge and left a message. She put an empty coffee can underneath the drip and knocked on the upstairs neighbours' door to find out if they were the cause of the leak. But she came down disheartened, informing Awoowe Rashid—who seemed so unconcerned you would have thought it was neither his home nor his issue—that she had personally checked their bathroom and their floors.

We ate dinner quietly. Hooya got up every ten minutes to check the leak, and I couldn't believe how engrossed she had become in Awoowe Rashid's life—in his problems. For the first time in a long time, my mother didn't feel so impermanent.

"KHALI, WAKE UP. We have to go back." My mother was leaning against my dresser, holding her mobile phone loosely. I could hear vaguely upbeat elevator music through the speakerphone. "I'm on hold. I'm trying to find someone to fix the leak. Get up."

It was Saturday. We never visited Awoowe Rashid on the weekend. We spent our weekends doing our own chores: stripping our beds and hanging the linens on the line outside. On Saturday, I got to play with the neighbourhood kids, and on Sunday, we went grocery shopping. I wanted to object to this odd disruption of our routine.

I met Hooya in the kitchen still in my pyjamas. "Khali," she said, exasperated. She was sitting with a cup of coffee.

Hooya pulled me towards her, took off my glasses, and held me tightly around the shoulders. "Please don't be difficult. I'm so nervous. What if Upti Rashid slips and breaks his hip? He could get really injured."

Hooya's pleading was enough to make me sit down to a bowl of oatmeal and then get dressed.

Hooya looked relieved when Awoowe Rashid came to his door holding the TV remote.

She patted his arm, asked how he had slept, and took a few strides into the hall to check on the leak. The coffee can was overflowing with water, and the drips were falling faster. On the ceiling, the sag had accumulated a swollen bubble of water, from which a fat droplet emerged and fell ceremoniously.

Hooya left another message for the property's designated emergency maintenance workers, who still had not gotten back to her or Awoowe Rashid. She was on the phone, trying to find another plumber, when they came on the line. She spoke to a man who said he was in the area and would drop by to assess the situation. She emptied the coffee can, wiped the floor with a hand towel, and then placed the coffee can on top of the towel. She made Awoowe Rashid a cup of tea and sat down. He was watching a Somali news broadcast transmitted from a special cable box. The program was covering a story on the conditions of the Dadaab refugee camp in Kenya. One man interviewed stated that he had lived there for fifteen years. He had arrived with his wife and children in 1993 and recently welcomed his first grandchild in the camp.

Awoowe Rashid shook his head. "They live there," he said, pointing to the TV with his remote. It was a desert. Aerial shots showed a sweep of sand and hundreds of tiny, white, dome-shaped tents.

Hooya clicked her tongue in sympathy. "Did you pass through Kenya?"

Awoowe Rashid was distracted by images of classrooms that were full of mostly Somali and South Sudanese students. "What did you say?"

"I asked if you passed through Kenya. Were you there?"

"Me?" He seemed offended. "No, thank God. I've never been there. I went to Ethiopia. Dire Dawa. I have relatives there."

"How long were you in Ethiopia?"

"Several years. Five or six."

"When did you come here, again?"

Awoowe Rashid looked at my mom with an exhausted expression and didn't answer right away. "1999."

"And how? You never told me. Did you seek asylum?"

"Did I what?"

Hooya sat forward, resting against the arm of the sofa. "Asylum. It's for people who can't go home because it's not safe. Because of wars. Is that what you did?"

"Do you work for the government?"

"No!" My mother laughed.

"But your job. It's a government job, right?"

"No, it's an agency. Like a small company. They get calls from people who need an interpreter and they send me or someone else."

"I thought it was some kind of government job."

"It's not a government job," Hooya assured him.

He shrugged and turned back to the television. In studio, a serious news anchor in an oversized suit jacket was interviewing a famous Somali singer who had been living quietly in Birmingham.

"Tell me, Upti Rashid. How did you come here in 1999?"

"My daughter brought me," he said, with a readiness Hooya seemed unprepared for.

"Your daughter?"

"Yes. Firdowsa."

"The older one? The one I spoke to yesterday?"

"Yes, her."

"But—how?"

"With her husband's passport. An American passport."

"Her husband's—ah. So you pretended to be her husband?"

His face revealed nothing. "We went from Dire Dawa to Doha. Doha to Amsterdam. We had one more flight to America, but they caught us here."

"That's incredible! They didn't send you back?"

"No. They wanted to. They held us and questioned us. Firdowsa explained the situation. She wouldn't leave until she knew what they would do with me. In the end, they agreed not to deport me. They gave me a room in a shelter. After a long time, they gave me this place."

"What about Firdowsa? Did she get in trouble?"

"Of course. It was a headache. She thought they would throw her in jail. But they gave her a warning and revoked her passport for ten years. She still can't travel."

We were interrupted by a loud knock on the door. The plumber greeted Hooya, followed her down the hall in his workboots, and touched the ceiling, wiping at the blob of water with a rag that was hanging from his back pocket. He said he would begin repairs on Monday because he had to purchase the right materials, and he warned the leak would probably get worse in the meantime.

Hooya nodded distractedly. She had a frantic expression on her face, like she was struggling to absorb information while her mind reeled. I reached for her, placing my hand on her thigh, but she startled and looked at me angrily. She made up a plate of leftovers for Awoowe Rashid and put it in the microwave for him to warm up later. I waited for her at the door, my resentment from earlier in the morning resurfacing.

In the car, I began to pick at my lips. "You were wrong," I blurted out.

Hooya clicked in her seat belt. "What did you say? Stop that, Khali."

I clasped my hands tight in my lap. "You thought Awoowe Rashid had bad children. You said they left him. But they didn't. He just told you."

"You were listening?"

I nodded.

My mother seemed pleased to know that I had been paying attention to their conversation. "You're right. Upti Rashid's children didn't forget about him. Firdowsa took a big risk to bring her father to the West, and it paid off. Even if he is here all alone, his life is better than it would've been if he'd stayed in Ethiopia. Do you understand?"

"Yes," I said.

But Hooya looked unconvinced. "No, you don't. You don't understand."

THE NEXT MORNING, I rubbed my eyes and reached for my glasses. I lay in bed, half-expecting Hooya to push open the door and order me to get dressed, but fifteen minutes passed and she didn't come. I realized that although my door was partly open, I couldn't hear my mother moving around the house. I called for her, but there was no answer. Her bedroom door, which she usually kept closed, was flung open and the light was on. A few of her thin summer cardigans had fallen off their hangers and were lying in a pile at the bottom of the wardrobe. I checked the bathroom and Faisal's room. I went downstairs, calling for her. Everything looked as it always did, but our car was not parked in front of the house. I checked the kitchen anyway, even opening the back door in case she was hanging laundry.

The phone rang and I rushed towards it.

"Khali! You won't believe it. I'm having the best time. Italy is beau—"

"Faisal! Hooya isn't here."

There was a lot of background noise on his end of the line. "Oh, all right. How are you doing?"

"I'm good," I said, exhaling. "But Hooya isn't here. She's not home."

"Is she at work?"

"No, it's Sunday. I woke up, and she's not *here*." I couldn't believe that Faisal didn't grasp my meaning.

"Okay, I'll try her mobile phone. But tell her I called. I'll be coming home soon."

He hung up before I could explain further, let alone say goodbye. I sat down, picking dead skin off my lips with my fingernails, holding the cordless phone in my other hand. I dialed Hooya's mobile number and it went straight to her voice mail. I tried again every two minutes until it finally began to ring, but there was still no answer. I brought my knees up and wrapped my arms around my legs. Perhaps she *had* gone to work? Or maybe she had gone to check on Awoowe Rashid? But why did she leave me alone in the house? Why not take me to the neighbour's, or along with her, like she always did? Had she finally done it? Had she actually deserted me?

I don't know how long I sat there. I didn't notice the car pull up or the key turn the lock in the door.

Toronto, 2011

AMIRA WAS STARING at the half-smiling, impersonal face of her ex-boyfriend, Yonis, in his Facebook profile picture when she heard the heavy creak of the glass door opening.

"Can I help you?" Amira said to the blond woman who entered, minimizing the browser on her desktop.

"Is he here?" she asked.

"Excuse me?"

"Brock. Is he here?" The woman peered around the corner where Brock's office was.

"He's on lunch," Amira said.

"I'm just getting my stuff." She went into the kitchenette, returned with a mug that read NAMASTE, and placed it on the side of Amira's desk. "Sorry," she said and opened the closet. Amira watched her closely. She left the closet door open, went back to the kitchenette, and returned with a plastic bag. She bent down, threw a pair of brown high-heeled loafers into the bag, and dropped the bag on the floor next to Amira's desk.

"I need to get in there," the woman said tersely. She went around the desk, reached over Amira — the limp, heat-damaged ends of her hair centimetres from Amira's face — and opened a low cupboard. Amira pushed her chair back. The woman grabbed two legal pads, one of which Amira had been using. From the bottom drawer, she took the June edition of *InStyle* magazine with Kerry Washington on the cover — Amira had already looked through it twice — and a pristine copy of *Sense and Sensibility*. She stacked them next to the NAMASTE mug and started towards Brock's office.

"Hey," Amira said, standing up, "you can't go in there. It's locked."

The woman ignored her. She tried the glass door and it opened. Through the glass walls, Amira could see her rummaging around Brock's desk. Amira grew uneasy, worried that Brock might return from his lunch break right at that moment and question them both. She lifted the phone off the receiver. The sticky note with his cellphone number was stuck to her desk, under some paperwork. She pushed the papers aside when the woman started walking towards her, holding up a silver ballpoint pen.

"This is mine," she said.

Amira put the phone down and looked at the pen carefully. "It has his name on it."

"I gave it to him," the woman said, drawing her hand back. "It was a gift."

Amira sat down again. "Are you done?" She wondered, annoyed, why Brock hadn't warned her about this disgruntled ex-employee who would return for her belongings.

The woman opened the canvas bag she held at her side and stuffed in the legal pads and magazine, followed by the book, the pen, and the mug. She pulled the straps of her bag tight against her shoulder and exhaled sharply. Then she looked around. "So what are you guys working on?"

Amira checked the time on her desktop. Brock had been gone for over an hour. "I'm legal admin," Amira said. The woman just stared at her, so she added, "He's got a few cases at the moment."

"Who helps him? Lee?"

"Yeah," Amira said. "Or Jared." She didn't know why she was telling the woman this.

The woman laughed, her mouth hanging open. "He hates them."

The phone rang. Relieved, Amira hoped the woman would slip out while she was on the call. BEVERLY MILLER appeared on the display.

"Bitch," the woman said under her breath.

Amira froze, and then recovered. "Excuse me?"

"Oh, not you," she said quickly. She nodded towards the ringing phone, and then turned her back to it.

Amira picked up. "Hi, Beverly."

"Is my husband in?"

"He's on lunch."

"Still?" It was 1:12 p.m.

Amira had only been out to lunch with Brock once, her first month on the job. He took her to the TASTE bistro on King Street West. The waitress was a small girl with a pixie haircut and flushed cheeks. She greeted Brock enthusiastically and slipped into small talk as she leaned against their table, ignoring Amira until Brock introduced her as his new assistant.

"Oh," the waitress said. "Hi!" And Amira could tell that whatever animosity the girl had felt—and pretended not to feel—had melted away.

They ordered and the waitress took their menus. Brock asked Amira how she was finding the office and if anyone was giving her a hard time. For the first two weeks, she had been drowning in paperwork because of the paralegals from down the hall who were constantly handing her folders with instructions.

Then one morning, Brock was hovering behind her, holding a coffee. He flipped through the papers on her desk. "Who told you to do this?"

She described the lanky paralegal who had brought her

the folder she was working on. She didn't know his name, but he wore glasses—Jared, she discovered. And then she picked up another large manila envelope, and another, and explained.

Brock drank the last of his coffee, dropped the paper cup into the wastebasket, gathered the papers, and walked out with the files.

He returned a few minutes later and said, "You don't have to do their work."

He was angry on her behalf, and this filled her with such gratitude and relief that she called her sister on her commute home to relay the events of her workday and found herself saying, "I love him! I love him!"

She knew the only reason Brock had taken her out to lunch was because the others on their floor had shunned her after that. And because, as far as Amira knew, they were the only Black people working at the firm, excluding some of the overtired cleaners she sometimes saw as she was leaving for the day.

Amira hung up the phone and scribbled Beverly's message with the time of her call and carefully ripped it from the message pad.

"Anything else?" Amira said to the blond woman, who was still standing before her. Do you want to leave Brock a message, too?"

"You're pretty," the woman said.

"Thanks," Amira said warily.

"Does he tell you that?"

"What?"

"Does he tell you you're pretty?"

"Listen—" Amira reached for some documents she had to photocopy, unclipped them, and rose. "I have to work."

The woman picked up the plastic bag that held her shoes. "I do have a message for him," she said.

Amira was at the door, holding it open. "Well, what is it?"

She stopped in front of Amira. "Tell him I said fuck you."

WHEN AMIRA GOT HOME she messaged Yonis.

Hey, I heard the news. Congrats!

Even though it was old news. Her friend Farhia had told her months ago that Yonis was engaged to some twenty-two-year-old girl from Jamestown. Farhia knew—because her little cousin was friends with the girl—how long they had been dating and when they would marry. Farhia had done her duty as a friend by gathering this information, and, naturally, she expected a thorough questioning in which she could relay the details bit by bit. But Amira didn't care, and she wondered why Farhia could not accept that Yonis had not deeply affected her. The truth was that theirs was a brief relationship, only five months of mostly phone calls and text messages and occasional dates, which would end with Amira feeling peeved at what she saw as Yonis's immaturity, and Yonis trying desperately to mitigate her growing discontent.

She hadn't bothered to congratulate him at the time. Amira was worn out from her previous job with the immigration lawyers on Eglinton, fed up with the long hours and the extra work and the dismal pay. She had mistakenly assumed—because it was a small office with a staff of only five—that her efforts would be visible and that a promotion would soon follow. The partners were brothers, both small and wiry with dishevelled hair and glasses. They depended on her to the point that they called her on her days off. She took pride in managing the office smoothly, in anticipating schedule conflicts and redirecting calls. She treated the clients with kindness and understanding because she saw herself reflected in them, whether they were from Sri Lanka or Benin or Romania. She had the impression, in the early days, that she was doing important work. That although she was only technically a legal clerk—really a glorified secretary—she was in the heart of a big machine that submitted applications and appealed court rulings and stalled deportations—all important acts—to keep a family together or ensure that a person, young or old, had a life to look forward to instead of being sent back to a place that they had deliberately left.

But after her twenty-fifth birthday, Amira had spent each day at work worrying that it would be her last — that she would snap and abruptly quit. Miraculously, she did not. She put away the files and shut down the computers and turned off the lights each afternoon. She was impressed and saddened by her own perseverance, until she heard about a position with one of the big law firms downtown. Amira applied, and then interviewed, and then finally gave her two weeks' notice and quit.

Yonis's response came fourteen minutes later.

Hey! Thanks! How have you been?

Amira stared at the words and took a deep breath. There was none of the anger or bitterness she felt she deserved. He was just as she remembered from three years ago, congenial and forgiving.

What was she doing? She turned off her phone and put it on the nightstand. She was thinking about Yonis a lot lately, ever since she began working for Brock. The dynamic between Brock and his wife — from the glimpses Amira had caught when Beverly stopped by — had felt familiar. Amira snuck glances as Beverly manoeuvred out of Brock's embraces or looked away when he gazed down at her, cupping her chin with his fingers. Beverly behaved like a woman who had become disillusioned with her own beauty, her own charm. Like someone who was bored of the effect they caused.

Amira could not have known, when she caught sight of Brock's wedding band at her interview, how often she would interact with his wife. Beverly stayed home in Richmond Hill with their two young children but managed — at least once a week and without any notice — to show up at the office. She had a subtle, lilting Caribbean accent and she was so beautiful, with her golden skin and prominent cheek-bones, that Amira could not help but admire them together. They were so equally attractive that it gave Amira an odd sense of satisfaction.

She decided to ask Lee about Beverly a couple days after her encounter with the blond ex-employee. Lee was dangling a pencil and holding a blue binder that looked full and organized while he waited around Amira's desk for Brock to finish a call.

"Hey, can I ask you something? You know Beverly, right?"

"Brock's wife?"

"Yeah," Amira said. "Has she — has she *always* come into the office?"

"Hm. I don't know. I guess after the whole Cassandra thing... Yeah, I mean, she comes around more now."

"What Cassandra thing? Who's Cassandra?"

"Oh, she was the girl before you. Paralegal. Did the office stuff, too. She was, like, Brock's right-hand man. Except — not a man." He laughed.

Amira smiled indulgently. So the blond woman—the disgruntled former employee—was Cassandra. "What happened?"

"Brock fired her. I don't know why. I mean, she was good at her job." Lee looked towards Brock's office. "From what I hear... she made him do it. Beverly. She wasn't comfortable with, uh, *Miss* Cassandra."

Amira wanted to know more, but Brock had ended his call and was waving Lee in. Lee tapped the edge of his binder on Amira's desk and smiled playfully, then he neutralized his face and hurried into Brock's office. Amira watched as he stood before Brock like a deferential pupil, his binder held against his abdomen, his left arm supporting it while he flipped through pages.

Amira had made sure to tell Brock about Cassandra when he'd returned from his lunch break. In case he suspected that someone had been in his office, she wanted him to know that it wasn't her. She told him about the pen. He nodded at her, seemingly in a rush to get back to work. She was heading towards her desk when she remembered to give him Beverly's message.

"Thanks, Amira. I'll get back to her."

When Amira had reopened her browser, she was startled to see Yonis's picture spread across her computer screen again. Only his upper body showed, his hands in the pockets of a black bomber jacket. He appeared wide-eyed and unsuspecting, like the photo was a candid. Really, Brock and Yonis were nothing alike. But Amira wondered if, in ten or fifteen years, Yonis would be as successful and accomplished as Brock. He was handsome and intelligent: a computer engineer with a university degree. He had even tried, when they were together, to gently goad Amira into going back to school. She would just have to upgrade her college diploma to an undergraduate degree, and then apply to law school. He said it like it was the easiest transition in the world, rather than one that would take four to five years and tens of thousands of dollars. Amira shrugged him off. The truth was she had never intended to have a career. She had naively assumed that she would get married right out of school, like so many girls she knew. Although her grades had been good enough for her to go to university, Amira had no real direction and was hesitant about committing to a four-year program. She began in Early Childhood Education, and then switched to Human Resources before settling on the Law Clerk program because — and she never admitted this — she loved watching *Law & Order*. She thought she might get just enough excitement from being at the periphery of what she imagined could only be high-profile case studies and legal precedents. She hadn't considered that when she finished her program, she wouldn't actually *want* to get married, so she ended things with Yonis via an angry text, and ignored his calls and messages when he tried to talk it through. She focused on securing a job, and when she started working for the immigration lawyers, she made a conscious effort to be organized and diligent. She had found fulfillment in her work, until she began to feel ill-used and burned out.

Now, working for Brock, some of that old self-importance had returned. Amira bought new pieces for her work wardrobe, mostly pencil skirts and button-up shirts and wide-leg slacks. She applied excessive amounts of leave-in conditioner to her hair so her curls looked shiny and tight, or she slicked it back into a clean bun with gel and a stiff bristle brush. Her makeup was usually natural. She could often get away with wearing just some concealer, powder, and mascara. She knew she was a pretty girl. She had to endure unwanted attention from men, not-so-subtle small talk that often led to a request for her phone number when she was commuting to work or buying a latte, and she made sure to walk the careful line of responding politely so as not to offend, while also keeping an air of aloofness. She never smiled at these strangers, but she always looked at them. She had heard a story about a girl whose face was slashed in the street with a pocket knife because she ignored a man who was hitting on her. Amira didn't know if it was a true story, but ever since hearing it, she adopted the habit of checking where men kept their hands. She was extremely wary of any man who kept his hands in his pockets.

~

AMIRA AGREED TO meet with Yonis. It had been three weeks since their text exchange. They had both been surface and cordial, wishing each other well. Then, one night, Yonis called Amira and confessed that even though he was engaged to be married in the summer, he wanted to see her.

Yonis picked her up the next Saturday. He looked a little dazed, a little nervous. He asked if Amira was hungry and suggested they get brunch instead of just the coffee they had decided on over the phone. He took her to a Denny's all the way in Woodbridge, and when she remarked on the distance he looked both apprehensive and resolved, so she just sat back and stared through the windshield.

In the Denny's, he relaxed. They were seated at a booth in the corner of the restaurant, at Yonis's request. There were only two other tables being served: a family with three adolescent children and an elderly couple who were eating in silence. Yonis asked what Amira had been up to, and she began to tell him about her new job, her boss, the kind of law he practised—corporate, which wasn't as banal as she had expected. Yonis was staring at her, continuously looking her up and down instead of holding her gaze. She could tell he was not interested in what she was saying. He asked if she was dating anyone, if she had dated anyone since their breakup.

She shrugged. "Here and there. Nothing serious."

He seemed relieved at this news. After they placed their orders and the waitress had walked away, he reached across the table for her hand.

"I miss how we used to hold hands. Can I hug you?" he asked hesitantly. "When I picked you up, we didn't hug."

"Okay," Amira said, laughing a little, but she remained seated while he rose, and he had to motion for her to get up. When she did, Yonis pulled her close, holding her, pressing his body against hers, burying his face in her neck. He had never hugged her like this before — so long and sensual. Amira thought he was going to start kissing her. She was sure he was pushing his crotch into her stomach. She broke away from him and sat down again. Yonis smiled and sat next to her, reaching again for her hand, which was in her lap. She slipped it away and crossed her arms.

He leaned towards her. "I'm just so attracted to you," he said. "Trust me, if I wasn't with my girl, I would try to make it work."

There was an unctuous quality to his tone, his gestures, his gaze, something that, at one time, Amira had recognized and found pathetic. She had assumed it was a by-product of the power she wielded over him. Now, she realized, it was being used against her. To lull her into some kind of shallow passion.

"Make what work?" Amira said.

"Us. You and me."

The waitress placed an Americano and a latte in front of them. The food would be out in just a minute, she said.

"Why did you want to see me?" Amira asked, getting irritated.

"I don't know. For closure, I guess?"

Amira fixed her eyes on him. He didn't need closure. She sat quietly, sipping at her latte.

"Don't you think it could've worked out between us?" he asked.

It struck Amira that she had been asking herself that same question. She shook her head. "We're not right for each other. I think we should've been friends."

This reply deflated him. "Friends? I never saw you as a friend."

The waitress was coming towards them with their plates. Yonis took his seat across from her again. They ate quickly and left.

In the car, he returned to an earlier version of himself, the version she had first met three years ago. He was easy-going and conversational. He remarked that she was a good girl and that he had a lot of respect for her. He mentioned his fiancée for the second time that morning.

"Wait, we didn't do anything wrong, right? We just hugged."

Amira was astounded that he would make her witness this false contemplation. "It felt wrong," she said.

Yonis shrugged and said he hoped she didn't think too badly of him. The way he was able to speak about what had happened not an hour before as if they were the foolish actions of a younger, immature, former self amazed Amira. There was none of the longing—the feral desire that had unexpectedly gripped him—in his countenance anymore. Yonis wished Amira the best and drove off.

AMIRA WAS LOOKING DOWN at the street through the floor-to-ceiling windows behind her desk while she ate apple slices from a Ziploc bag. It was a bright day and the little snow that had been on the ground had melted. Traffic was steady. Pedestrians appeared miniature. She heard the door open and turned to see Beverly entering the office.

"Hey," Beverly said, pushing her sunglasses back. She looked into Brock's office.

"Oh—" Amira covered her mouth as she finished chewing a bite of apple. "Hi Beverly." She dropped the plastic bag onto her desk. "Brock's out to lunch."

"Of course he is. When did he leave?"

Amira sat down and looked at the time on her desktop. "Maybe fifteen minutes ago? Did you try calling him?"

"No." Beverly sighed. "I was hoping to catch him before he left so we could have lunch together."

"You just missed him."

Beverly went to the window where Amira had been standing. "What about you? Have you eaten yet? I know a good place."

Amira was happy to join Beverly for lunch. They ended up in front of the TASTE bistro on King Street West, where they were greeted by the waiter, who led them to a table and brought them menus, which Beverly didn't even glance at. Instead, she looked around the restaurant and got up to find the restroom. A minute later, she returned, seeming disappointed. She hooked her Givenchy bag onto her chair and took off her jacket. She ordered a caprese salad and garlic bread, then sent some messages from her BlackBerry.

When the food came, Beverly became more talkative. "What does 'Amira' mean"? she asked.

"It's Arabic for 'princess,'" Amira said. She had loved the meaning of her name as a child, but the older she got, the more it embarrassed her.

Beverly smiled and exclaimed, "How adorable! My mother named me after the city. Beverly Hills. Spelled the same way, too."

Amira's eyes widened. "Really?"

"I know." Beverly smirked, holding a tomato slice in the air on her fork. "She put me in pageants since I was a little girl."

Amira couldn't imagine Beverly as a little girl. She was so refined and self-possessed.

"I was Miss Bermuda, you know." Beverly ate the tomato slice.

"No way!"

She rolled her eyes and waved her fork dismissively. "That was a long time ago."

Beverly insisted on paying the bill, and they walked back to the office together, but Brock still hadn't returned from his break. Finally, Beverly left.

For the rest of the week, Brock promptly returned from lunch within a half hour. When Amira went to put his mail on his desk that Friday, he asked her if it was okay if he gave Beverly her email address.

"She's really into this party she's planning. I don't even know what the occasion is, but—" he squinted at her— "you're invited."

It occurred to Amira that Brock did not know about her lunch with Beverly. Or about all the calls she fielded when he was in meetings, or on the phone, or out to lunch, which she had stopped documenting on the message pad or even telling him about because they were so frequent, and because Amira soon perceived that Beverly, rather than actually wanting to speak to Brock, simply wanted to know where he was or what he was doing.

The next week, Brock went back to taking his full lunch hour. Amira saw the invitation in her inbox. She clicked the link and RSVP'd. A few minutes later, Beverly called the office phone. "It's just a dinner party!" she demurred. "For ten, maybe twelve, guests, max. You could come straight over with Brock after work. He doesn't get home until around seven anyway, and the party starts at eight. That's if you don't mind hanging around a little bit. I'll make sure you get a ride home with one of the guests heading back into the city. Just wear something a little formal. Not too much, a dress or a skirt—something like that. It'll be fun, I promise."

Amira was excited. She had never been to a dinner party.

The next day, Brock went out for lunch at noon. Amira had planned to eat a fruit cup at her desk, but she wanted to try the caprese salad that Beverly had ordered. The girl who placed her takeout order was the same petite, short-haired waitress that had been rude to her when Brock had first brought her to the bistro for lunch. Her cheeks were still flushed, but her hair was even blonder. She was curt and hurried, even though the restaurant wasn't particularly busy.

Amira decided to eat her lunch in the park. On her way back to the office, with her earbuds in to listen to music, Amira distractedly missed her turn. She took a side street and saw the familiar figure of a man's back up ahead. She kept walking until she noticed he was embracing a woman, whose face Amira couldn't see because it was tucked into his neck, but whose stringy blond hair she intuitively recognized. Amira stopped, turned around, walked back up the street, and turned the corner. She stood there for a moment, breathing heavily, her mind racing. Then she cautiously peered from behind the small brick storefront that was concealing her. The woman had lifted her face and was smiling, though, even from afar, Amira could tell she was upset. She let go of the man and wiped at her eyes. He looked around, and Amira saw his profile. Brock pulled Cassandra towards him again and kissed her.

AFTER FINISHING WORK on Friday, Amira went into the women's restroom and changed into her party outfit. She wore a new gold-speckled, calf-length dress. She paired the dress with a cropped black cardigan, touched up her makeup, put on some dangly gold earrings, and pinned the front half of her hair up into a bun.

When she got back to her desk, Brock raised both hands to indicate he'd be done in ten minutes. Amira shut down her computer and waited. Her stomach was in knots. She wasn't looking forward to the dinner party anymore. She suddenly wanted to keep a professional distance from both Brock and his wife. She felt pity, not for Beverly exactly — she was too formidable. Rather, Amira felt sorry for the conclusions she had drawn, for the way she had regarded Beverly's behaviour as slightly paranoid, controlling, possessive, instead of warranted.

"Let's go," Brock said.

He led her to a silver Maserati in the building's under-ground parking and surprised her by opening her door.

"Traffic is going to be brutal," Brock said. "Be prepared."

Amira worried that the ride might be long and uncom-fortable, but she had forgotten how Brock had always gone out of his way to be kind to her. He asked about her daily commute and about her family, if the news reports he'd heard about Somalia were accurate and if she'd ever visited. He hadn't taken a trip back home until he was sixteen, he told her. His grandmother, who had raised him and retired to Anguilla, had been sick and he'd wanted to visit her.

"Man, it was beautiful," he said wistfully. "I mean, this is nice —" he motioned to the skyscrapers they were passing on the highway — "but there's nothing like being home."

They discussed their national dishes, office politics, and what parts of the city they'd lived in. It was like talking with a distant relative who was visiting from out of town, and who you knew, once they left, you would not talk with so intimately again.

When they pulled up to Brock's house there was one car in the driveway and a white van with MARIE LOUISE'S CATERING SERVICES on the side in swirly blue letters parked next to the curb. Brock parked in the garage and led Amira through a mud room — where she left her work bag and pulled out a multicoloured Michael Kors clutch — and past the kitchen, where cooks in chef's uniforms were busily mixing and chopping and opening oven doors.

"This way," Brock said. He guided Amira to the formal sitting room. "Have a seat. Make yourself comfortable. I'm sure someone will be here with a drink or something. I'm just going to clean up."

He went through the hall and up the staircase. Amira sat down in an ornate, upholstered wingback chair. She had a view of large bay windows, which were covered by tufted, eggshell-blue drapes with silver tassels. There was an antique-looking armoire in the corner and a long white table against the back of the large ivory sofa. She got up and walked around the sofa. Along the table there was a row of framed photos, along with animal figurines — an elephant, a giraffe, a dolphin — and matching vases with fresh white tulips on both ends. The picture in the centre was a wedding photo. Beverly was wearing a strapless ball gown and her black hair was tied back in an elaborate updo. She was holding on to Brock's arm and looking into the camera austerely. Brock's hands were in his tuxedo pockets, and he had a wide grin on his face — a smile so big he must have been mid-laugh when the photo was taken. It occurred to Amira that she had never seen Brock give more than a polite smile, though he had perfect teeth. She marvelled at how happy he looked. The two pictures on either side were family portraits, one of them taken in a park, the other a more recent Christmas photo taken by the stairs. Amira examined the Christmas portrait—they looked like the family of a politician. Their daughter was about eight or nine years old in the photo, standing in front of her father in a ruffled black-and-white dress, while their son, who was six, stood before Beverly in a bespoke suit. A framed photo on the end showed Beverly sitting in a red armchair, wearing a glittery lilac spaghetti-strap dress, a diamond-encrusted silver crown, and a sash that read MISS BERMUDA.

Feeling uneasy, Amira wandered off to find the powder room, and then sat down on the settee by the bay windows. Her spot gave her a good view of the whole room and the staircase.

Fifteen minutes later, a man in a black vest and bow tie came into the room with a tray and said, "Champagne, miss?"

"No, thanks." It dawned on Amira that she would be around people who were drinking. All her friends were Somali girls, who, at most, smoked hookah and, occasionally, if they could get it, weed. Whenever she had seen drunk people in restaurants, on the street at night, or the few times she went clubbing, she was struck by the strong, sour smell of the alcohol, the uninhibited and volatile ways people behaved, and how that might encroach upon her sober bubble of superiority.

"Can I get you something else, miss?"

Amira asked for sparkling water and sniffed the champagne glass it was served in before taking a sip. Beverly came down the stairs wearing a sleeveless leopard-print jumpsuit with a big belt cinching her waist. Her hair hung dead straight down her back. She smiled at Amira and walked towards her with open arms.

"Thank you so much for coming," she said as she hugged her.

"Thanks for having me," Amira said, steadying her champagne glass as she came out of the hug. "Um, your home is beautiful."

Beverly smiled, looking towards the kitchen. "I knew you would be early, but I hope you weren't too bored."

"No, no."

"Let me just check on things." She touched Amira lightly on the arm and left the room.

The guests began to arrive, greeted by the waitstaff. Each one beamed and walked towards Amira as if they knew her, reaching for her hand and asking her to repeat her name. She was captivated by the guests, all of them some shade of brown, glowing, at ease. There was a dreadlocked documentarian from Brooklyn and his pregnant girlfriend who was working on her Ph.D. at the University of Toronto. There was a South African man who worked as a physiotherapist for the Toronto Argonauts and a

Bangladeshi gynecologist who was a neighbour and close friend of Beverly's. The only white people were the servers, the cooks, and an elderly man with an Irish accent whom Brock introduced to Amira as his favourite law professor when he had attended Osgoode.

Amira soon forgot her trepidation and found herself relaxing in the company of the dinner guests, who fascinated her and also flattered her with their specific attentions. The night was magical. She felt present, alert—but there was another part of her that felt wistful, hyperaware that what she was feeling would escape her soon enough, and that she would not even have the words to describe it. She was sitting on the sofa with Beverly's cousin Sonya, who was a blogger, and the Ph.D. student. Sonya had written a post about healing from a breakup, and Amira was listening attentively, her chin resting on her hand. In any other circumstance, she would find it bizarre and somewhat embarrassing to be engaged in such a personal conversation with someone she hardly knew, but somehow, the dim lighting and the beautiful furniture and the unintelligible chatter in the background, mixed with Sonya's earnestness, allowed Amira to nod along, while slightly lost in her own thoughts about Yonis and his fiancée and the way he had pressed against her in the Denny's.

Out of the corner of her eye, Amira registered a petite blond woman standing by the bay windows. She recognized her instantly: the waitress from the bistro was standing with her arms crossed, sipping from a champagne glass and staring brazenly in Brock's direction. Amira was confused. The waitress wasn't dressed for the party. She was wearing a corduroy miniskirt and a baseball shirt. Amira looked at Brock, who was sitting in a corner, engaged in a loud discussion with his old law professor and the documentarian. She scanned the room for Beverly and, when she couldn't find her, excused herself to approach the girl.

"Hey," Amira said.

"Hey."

"I'm Amira." She held out her hand. "I don't know if you remember me? I work for Brock, at Hulche, Roberts, and DiGrazio."

"Oh, okay." The girl shook Amira's hand.

"Are you looking for someone?" Amira asked.

The girl seemed taken aback. "Um, kind of."

"What are you doing here?" Amira said, aware that her tone was interrogative.

"Excuse me?"

Amira stepped closer and lowered her voice. "Why are you here?" She didn't want to make a scene.

The girl stepped back. "That's *noooone* of your business."

Then Beverly appeared from behind Amira and said, "Lucy, come this way." She led the girl towards the hall. Amira watched as Beverly unzipped a monogrammed

Louis Vuitton wallet, handed the girl a one-hundred-dollar bill, thanked her, and walked her out. Amira sat down on the settee, feeling stupid and disoriented.

Beverly returned and sat down next to her. "Were you intimidating my babysitter?" she said with amusement.

Amira shook her head self-consciously. "I'm so sorry, Beverly. I didn't know you knew her. I thought she wasn't supposed to be here." Amira sighed, and then added, "She works at the TASTE bistro by the office."

"I know." Beverly was quiet for a while, and Amira couldn't read her expression. "Look at Brock," she finally said.

Amira had a clear view of him, and she perceived a subtle look of discomfort unlike any she recalled ever seeing on his face. Brock always appeared dignified, in control. Now, he looked sweaty, distracted, and altogether pitiful.

"Is he okay?" Amira asked, mildly concerned.

"Oh, he'll be fine," Beverly said. "He almost *fainted* when he saw her upstairs with the kids." She gave Amira a pleased, knowing look. "But he collected himself. He always does."

Amira stared at Beverly.

"You're wondering how I know?"

A waiter holding a napkin over his forearm stood at the entryway and announced that dinner was ready to be served. The guests rose slowly.

"There was another white girl before this one," Beverly continued, still seated. "and she's more jealous than I am."

Amira kept staring at her, flabbergasted.

"Well, I got rid of Cassandra. And I'll get rid of this one, too." Beverly stood up, smiling at the guests who were walking past her towards the dining room.

Amira stood up as well. She felt dizzy. She watched Brock and the old professor file past. Brock's top shirt button was undone and Amira could see perspiration by his temples. *Yonis would not sweat like that,* she thought resentfully. He would go on to marry that poor, clueless girl from Jamestown. But Beverly was under no illusions. She knew exactly who Brock was.

Yet—the image of Brock and Cassandra embracing in the street just the day before was still fresh in Amira's mind. She caught Beverly's wrist, causing her to look at Amira expectantly, and soon as Brock disappeared into the dining room, she said, "Beverly, I have to tell you something."

Dubai, 2016

THE MOMENT THE plane lands, my dread returns. The Egyptian woman next to me has unbuckled her seat belt even before the seat belt sign turns off. Her husband is muttering to her in Arabic. I'm assuming he's instructing her to get up quickly to stand in line. I sit, my head leaning against the window, my eye mask still on. I hear the bustle of movement: suitcases knocking against headrests, impatient groans, and children asking annoying questions until the drum of noise disappears completely.

"Excuse me, miss. Miss, excuse me. We've landed in Dubai."

When I take off my eye mask and look around, the plane is deserted. It's just me and the flight attendants standing at the back and the front of the plane.

I linger in the terminal for an hour before passing

through customs. I sit on a bench and take my iPhone off airplane mode. I play *Candy Crush* and pass four levels. Finally, I stand up and join a line. The customs officer is a young Emirati woman. Her makeup is thick. I think she looks terrible, but I've been staring at her so obviously that I ask her what blush she uses after she stamps my passport. When I make it to the baggage claim, a small Filipino man is taking my mother's beat-up purple suitcase off the conveyor. I tell him it's mine and wheel it through the arrivals gate. Almost immediately, I spot Habaryar Filsun. She's on the phone, but she sees me and waves frantically, the black sleeve of her abaya flapping in front of her. Habaryar Filsun hugs me briefly, and then passes me the phone. "It's Zainab," she states loudly, taking my suitcase and ushering me across the cool white tiles of the airport.

"Hello?" I say, but my mother has hung up. I hand back Habaryar Filsun's phone and keep walking, my hijab slipping off my head.

"Don't you have a pin?" Habaryar Filsun asks, looking back at me.

I pull it off, exposing my flattened dark hair, which is coming undone from its bun at the nape of my neck. Habaryar Filsun stops abruptly to glare at me in outrage or embarrassment; I can't tell.

I quickly place the scarf on the crown of my head, fold the sides, and wrap it tight around my neck. "Haye, there we go."

We spend the drive home making forced small talk. Habaryar Filsun tells me I will be sharing a room with her only daughter, Zahra, who is twelve. Habaryar Filsun's three boys have big heads and beady eyes, and they watch me when we arrive at the apartment with smirks on their faces, as if they know all about me. But Zahra is sweet. After everything I say, she asks, "Is it?" The third time, I respond, quite emphatically, "It is!" — as if she's questioning me. Then I realize it's just her British way of speaking. Her room is nice. It's painted a pale pink, and there are two twin beds, one against each wall, with a white nightstand in between. There is an AC unit above the door and a window that looks out into a little garden. I figure I could spend most of my time in this room.

HABARYAR FILSUN MOVED her family from London to Dubai only the year before. When my mother first suggested visiting, I said absolutely not. I don't know Habaryar Filsun well, but she's always forwarding me Islamic videos on WhatsApp and lecturing me about learning the Quran whenever we talk on the phone. She strikes me as the pushy religious type who has nothing to say if they can't admonish you. But then my brother came into the kitchen and opened the fridge. "Must be nice," he said. "After everything, you get a vacation to Dubai." I was eating cereal at the table instead of in my bedroom, and I was in one of my quiet moods, which scares my mother. And I thought, really, I might as well take advantage of whatever opportunities come my way. My mother booked my flight that week.

I sit on the twin bed and notice the firmness of the mattress. Despite this, I lie down and drift off to sleep.

I wake to Zahra pushing me gently on the shoulder. "Casho is ready," she says.

I follow her to the open living space. There is a dining table at one end with a clear view of the television, which is broadcasting a soccer game. The boys are seated at the table, watching the game, and Habaryar Filsun calls for Zahra, who goes back and forth, bringing dishes of food from the kitchen.

I look at Abdi-Karim, who is seated next to me. He has a pronounced overbite and his upper lip protrudes. "Why aren't you helping?" I say.

He looks at me, unsure whether I'm talking to him.

"Yeah, you," I say. "Why aren't you helping your sister?"

"Helping with what?" He already sounds offended.

"Setting the table," I say quietly, because the younger boy has noticed our conversation and is peering at me inquisitively, as if waiting to report back to his mother. "Don't you live here? My God!"

They both turn away and ignore me, which is fine with

me. Zahra finally sits down, and I give her a big smile to show I appreciate her. Habaryar Filsun also takes a seat. She is wearing a green and red patterned baati that drags across the rug and lies in folds at her feet. She smells like suugo, even though she's cooked rice and lamb — not pasta — and made a salad with boiled eggs. The food is very good.

"So how old *are* you?" Abdi-Majid asks. He's the youngest.

"Warya! Eat your food," his mother snaps. She's focused on a piece of lamb in her left hand, picking the meat off the bone with her right.

"I'm twenty-seven," I say proudly.

"*Twenty*-seven? Holy," Abdi-Majid says.

"Twenty-seven and you're not *married*?" Abdi-Nur asks. He's fourteen and the eldest. He seems both childish and domineering.

"Yes. I'm not married," I say, taking a drink of Fanta. "Should I go and kill myself?"

The table falls silent, and I notice Abdi-Nur's eyes shake as he looks down at his plate.

Habaryar Filsun puts down her meat. "What did I say?" she yells. "What did I say! Apologize to your cousin right now!"

"Sorry," Abdi-Nur mumbles.

Nobody talks for the rest of the meal.

≈

THAT NIGHT, I take a risk and smoke a cigarette through Zahra's bedroom window. There's no screen, so I slide the window all the way open and lean my upper body on the sill. Their apartment is on the second floor, and I can see somebody else's terrace below. I could jump and survive— I could sneak out, if I had anywhere to go and anybody to stop me from leaving. The door opens and I make sure to keep my cigarette out of view. Zahra closes the door and sits down on her bed.

"You're smoking," she says in an awed whisper.

I take a drag and blow it out into the night air. "Mhmm. Sue me."

She gives a puzzled laugh. "I'm not gonna sue you."

"Listen," I say, half-turning towards her. "I don't care if you tell your mom." I turn back to the window.

"Oh no—" she has her hands up, shaking them in front of her—"I'm not like *them*. I promise you."

"Like who?" I put out my cigarette on the outer brick wall and throw it away.

"The *boys*. They run and tell Mummy every little thing."

I leave the window open and take my Miss Dior perfume out of my suitcase. It's almost empty. I spray myself and the room, and then set it on the nightstand.

I climb into bed. "I think we'll get along, Zahra," I say, turning over and covering my head with the blankets.

The next morning, I wake up to an empty apartment.

I walk through the kitchen and the living room, peeking my head down the hall to the other two bedrooms, and decide to smoke. I'm digging around in my purse for my open pack of Belmonts when I hear a thud. I notice that the bathroom door is closed, but light is peeking through the cracks and the water is running. I knock.

A small girl with long, dark eyebrows opens the door. I stare at her. She doesn't speak. She's holding a Vim spray bottle in one hand and a blue rag in the other. I step back against the wall and notice that we're wearing the same baati. Habaryar Filsun left five — washed and ironed — on my bed when I arrived, and I instinctively reached for the black one first. It has a yellow pattern in the centre that reminded me of those psychological ink blot tests. It seemed fitting.

"Hi," I say.

"Habaryar left. She'll be back soon," the girl says wearily in Somali. "Do you want breakfast?"

"No, no. I'm okay," I say in Somali, too, hyperaware of my accent.

I sit at the little table tucked into the corner of the kitchen and play *Candy Crush* on my phone. I want a cup of coffee, but I don't see a coffee machine and don't want to poke around. About fifteen minutes later, the girl comes in, washes her hands, and then sits down across from me. She takes a banana out of the fruit basket on the table, peels it, breaks off pieces, and sticks them in her mouth.

"You're from Canada?" she asks.

I nod. "My name is Rabiya."

"I'm Muna. Nice to meet you," she says flatly. I wonder what she knows about me.

"You work here?" Now I recall hearing my mother boast to her friends that Habaryar Filsun had a house girl and barely lifted a finger.

"Yes," Muna says, chewing. "But only three days. I work at another house the other days. A big house."

I want to ask her for coffee, but I'm afraid to order her around.

"What about you?" she says. "What do you do in Canada? Are you studying at university?"

I wonder if this is a loaded question, but she seems both earnest and disinterested. "Oh, I'm finished."

She stares at me, waiting for me to go on. "What did you study?" she finally asks.

"I'm a nurse," I say.

Her eyebrows rise just enough for me to know that she believes me. "Mashallah," she says, getting up and throwing the banana peel in the trash can.

I feel not just relief but also a sweeping sense of self-satisfaction.

~

ON SATURDAY, HABARYAR FILSUN drives us all to the Dubai Mall in her Honda Pilot. She's surprised I agreed to come. The day before, she tried to get me up and ready for Jumah. She said the mosque was magnificent—built from white marble. But I spent most of the day in bed and only came out to eat. The boys, after they returned, looked at me suspiciously. As though they could not believe that refusing to go to the Friday prayer was an option.

Habaryar Filsun tells me that my mother has sent her money for my shopping. This is news to me. "How much?" I ask. She grabs Abdi-Majid's hand and doesn't answer. I walk aimlessly through the mall and notice they're all following me.

"What about this store?" Habaryar Filsun says, standing in front of H&M.

I wander through the women's section, flicking through hangers of hoodies.

"This is nice." Habaryar Filsun is holding up a bright orange maxi-skirt. "What size do you wear?"

"I don't like it," I say. "The colour." I start walking to the other side of the store, where there are dress shirts and other clothes I would never wear, just to get away from Habaryar Filsun.

"It comes in brown, and black," she says. "Come here. Look."

The boys have wandered off, but Zahra is standing by

her mother, feeling the fabric of the brown skirt. I take it from Habaryar Filsun's hands. "Hmm," I say, pretending to deliberate.

"What size do you wear?" She is leafing through the skirts on the rack, checking the tags.

"Uh, fourteen," I say.

Habaryar looks at me. "Are you sure?"

"Yeah. American fourteen. Maybe sixteen now. I don't know."

"Okay, here," she says, pulling out a size sixteen brown maxi-skirt. It seems significantly bigger than the skirt I'm holding. I check the label of the skirt in my hands. It's a size eight. Habaryar Filsun stares at the two skirts. "You should lose some weight," she says off-handedly.

I glare at her. She's at least twice my size. "*You* should lose some weight."

Her mouth drops open. "I'm—I'm a grown woman," she finally says. "I've had kids." She looks injured.

I put the skirt back on the rail. "Habaryar, just give me the money. I'll do my own shopping." I catch sight of myself in a mirror a few feet away, standing there with my hand on my hip, and I'm grateful for the enveloping blackness of the abaya I'm wearing—the one my mother bought me for Eid last year—which has little pearl buttons down the front and wide sleeves, and which I can wear comfortably over my leggings.

Habaryar Filsun opens her purse reluctantly, pulls out

an envelope, and hands me three five-hundred-dirham bills. "Where should we meet?" she asks.

I haven't bought a local SIM card yet, so I can't call her when I'm finished. "How about the entrance we came in from? In about two hours?"

She nods timidly.

"Or I can message you on WhatsApp. Using the Wi-Fi here." I smile, hoping she might feel that we've smoothed things over.

I leave H&M and take an escalator up to the second level. Zahra is right behind me, holding on to the handrail. She laughs exaggeratedly, bowed over, her other hand on her knee.

I get off the escalator and wait for her. She walks off to the side, to the second-storey railing, still laughing. "I can't believe you said that," she says.

Twenty-five minutes later, we're standing in line at Shake Shack. I tell Zahra to order whatever she wants. She's very excited. I'm wearing brand new Versace sunglasses I just purchased from the Sunglass Hut. I have 240 dirhams left, which is more than enough for our takeout.

While we wait for our order, I stand in front of a potted palm tree. "Take my picture," I say, handing Zahra my phone. "Up to here," I say, hitting my waist with the edge of my hand. I make her move about ninety degrees so I can get more light, then check the photos. "Not bad."

I take the phone back from Zahra and we collect our food. I start with the cheese fries, but Zahra is already taking big bites of her burger. She smirks. "The boys are going to be so jealous," she says, wiping ketchup off the side of her mouth with a napkin.

I contemplate sending one of my pictures to Najma, but we're not friends anymore. I scroll through the photos again while I eat my fries, and then I delete all of them.

EVERY EVENING AROUND SEVEN, when the kids are sitting at the table after dinner doing their homework, I go back to the bedroom and Zahra stands guard while I have a smoke. I know I should probably wait a few hours until everyone is asleep, but I can't. Tonight, I wait a while by the window, but there's no sign of Zahra. When I go out to see what's going on, Abdi-Karim and Abdi-Majid are at the table, books open, pencils in hand, though their eyes are on the TV. Abdi-Nur is playing FIFA on the PS4.

"Why aren't you doing your homework?" I say, standing behind the loveseat with my arms crossed.

Abdi-Nur doesn't take his eyes off the screen. "Don't have none," he says coolly.

Zahra's in a bad mood. She has a report due for her science class, but Habaryar Filsun is in her bedroom getting ready to attend a welcome dinner for an elderly woman who has just landed in Dubai from Sweden, so Zahra has to put the food away and load the dishwasher. When I come into the kitchen, she's scraping spaghetti off a plate and into the garbage with a fork. She has stacked the dirty pots on the stovetop, and the trash can is filled to the brim with onion skins, remnants of salad, chicken bones, and soiled paper towels. I fill the sink with hot water and squeeze the Sunlight detergent in a circle. We clean up together in less than thirty minutes.

When we're done, Habaryar Filsun comes out of her room in a showy bejewelled abaya that is open to a purple and navy-blue diraac. She's carrying her purse and a gift bag with multicoloured balloons printed on it. Her phone is tucked to her ear, held in place by her hijab, as she describes her gift — an expensive oud set — to the person on the line. She leaves without even acknowledging the clean kitchen.

Back in the bedroom, I finally have my cigarette and Zahra pulls the nightstand out in front of her to use as a desk. She's done all her research at school and shows me her neat notes, along with articles and photos she's printed off the internet and kept in the folder of her binder. The report is supposed to take the form of a travel brochure. Zahra pulls out a charcoal-grey sheet of construction paper she had rolled up in her backpack and carefully folds it in thirds.

"Did you get to choose your planet?" I ask.

"Uh-huh," she says, cutting around the bold letters of the word MERCURY from a magazine article headline.

"Why did you choose Mercury?"

"Why not?" she says.

"I don't know. Why not Mars? Or Saturn? Those are the big ones, right?"

She tilts her head, as if to consider my point. "Mercury is the smallest."

"What's so good about that?"

"It's *also*...closest to the sun."

"Hmm." I stub out my cigarette and chuck it out the window.

"Annnnd...it has a weird orbit."

"What does that mean?"

"The way it circles around the sun...I don't know, it's just weird. It's different from the other planets." She shuffles through a few pages in her binder. "See. It says right here: 'Mercury is famous for and unique in its orbital eccentricity.'" She shrugs after that offering and goes back to cutting and pasting.

I lie on the bed and scroll through my phone. I have the urge to talk to somebody, but I have no one to call. It's 6:48 a.m. in Ottawa. My mother is asleep, and she wouldn't want to hear from me anyway. This is as much a break for her as it is for me.

Najma would ordinarily be the first person I would reach out to when bored, frustrated, or lost. I miss her so much. I open my Gmail app and type painstakingly at first, but soon the words just come to me, and I have to get them down quickly to keep up with my train of thought.

From: Rabiya Farah

To: Najma Saleh

Subject: I'm Sorry...

Hi, I know you probably don't want to hear from me but I'm in Dubai, and I'm doing a lot of thinking and it's true what you said. My life is a mess. But I don't try to blame other people. I think I actually like to use people to distract me from this, which is why I was always dropping by your place. I didn't think I needed to give you notice. I mean, we've known each other since we were fourteen. But I get it, you're married now and you have a baby (Mashallah) and it's not just *your* house. I've just been feeling very confused and lonely. I know we're not seventeen anymore but I didn't think life would be like this. Did you? And I know what I said was wrong. I don't really believe you trapped Mustaf. I hate that I used something you told me in confidence against you. I didn't mean to throw it in your face but what did you expect? I failed my nursing exam for the third time and you were the only person I could tell and you threw that in my face.

Anyway, I understand if you don't want to be friends anymore. I just thought you still deserved this apology so I'm sorry.

Rabiya

I hit send hastily, before I change my mind. I look over at Zahra, who is carefully making a bullet list of interesting facts about Mercury in clear, loopy cursive. One of the younger boys cries out in a prolonged whine.

"Pfft," Zahra says, keeping the other panels of the construction paper flat with her right forearm. "They're probably not doing *any* work."

I get up and sit next to her. "Don't mind them," I say in a gentle tone that surprises me. "How can I help you?"

IT'S FRIDAY AGAIN. I wake up early, sneak a smoke, and then spray myself with perfume. Everyone is asleep, so I try to move around the apartment noiselessly. I hear the lock turn in the door. Muna greets me with an uninterested nod. She leaves her bag in the closet and opens the curtains in the living room. Soon, she's disappeared down the dark and quiet hall. I brush my teeth and use the mouthwash I asked Habaryar Filsun to buy as an extra precaution. I fill the kettle, turn it on, and grab a mug from the dishwasher. I've gotten quite used to the Nescafé instant coffee packets. I sit down at the kitchen table with my steaming cup and decide that I want to go to Jumah prayer. I don't know why. I just feel like this one prayer could shift things for me.

The masjid sits around the corner from Habaryar Filsun's apartment building, so we don't take the van. On the sandy sidewalks, boys and men in impeccable white thobes walk leisurely towards the small white mosque as the muezzin calls us to prayer. There are women, too, shuffling along, their long, black abayas collecting dust as they drag behind them. We separate from the boys, who enter the men's door on the side of the masjid. We climb a few stone steps, and I take my shoes off, placing them in the cubby next to Zahra's. Past the entry hall is a dramatic archway, with an ornately crafted red wooden door, the handles two big brass rings. *Here is an opening*, and I think of the Fatiha prayer. As I walk in, my bare feet feel the plushness of the carpeting that still retains some of the marks of a recent vacuuming. I pray the sunnah and sit in a corner, overwhelmed.

The last time I was in a masjid was when my mother tricked me a few weeks ago. I had locked myself in my room for a few days, I wouldn't speak to anyone, and I only went downstairs to make a sandwich or a bowl of cereal, leaving the dirty dishes on the floor next to my bed. Then my mother asked me what I wanted from the grocery store. She said I might as well go with her and pick out what I wanted myself; I might as well get some fresh air. And I believed her because she had said nothing about my dirty dishes or all the sandwiches I was making. I thought that it was a kind of peace offering—that she was going to leave me alone. I thought everyone was going to leave me alone for a little while. But instead, we pulled up to the mosque and she abruptly told me to get out. The imam was standing by the entrance, and I still didn't get it. I followed her inside, where they sat me down and covered me with a white sheet. The imam sat before me on a foldable chair that bent under his weight with a Quran open in his hands and started reading Surah Al-Baqarah, the longest chapter, in a booming voice. Terrified, I tried to get up, but my mother held me down. Without faltering in his recitation, the imam motioned to someone, and a young man came up from behind me and held me down, too. No matter how hard I fought, I could barely move. I couldn't believe that my mother had done this to me, and I started to sob. While I cried, my whole body heaved and convulsed. I bent my head so I could wipe away the tears that were blurring my vision and it became evident to me how the imam and my mother and this young man— who in other circumstances I would have tried very hard to impress—saw me. To them, I looked crazy. So I decided to be very still and quiet.

After a few more minutes, the young man let go of me and stepped away, and my mother, glancing back at him warily, let me go as well. Then I smiled, because I wanted to show the imam and my mother that I found the verses of the Quran to be very beautiful and moving, even though I didn't understand them. That, I figured, was the appropriate reaction. But I saw that I was making the imam uncomfortable by holding his gaze, so I gave up and started crying and thrashing again. He jumped up, causing the chair to fall behind him, and motioned again for the young man, who approached steadily with a bowl. The imam raised his voice even louder, dipping his fingers into the bowl and flicking zamzam water at me. I finally grew tired and stopped fighting, letting the holy water camouflage the tears running down my face.

AFTER MAGHRIB, HABARYAR FILSUN proposes we go to the beach. The younger boys jump up and crowd their mother, their large eyes looking even bigger with excitement. They change into swim trunks and grab a soccer ball. Before long we are at the Sharjah beach, not too far from the Pizza Hut. Habaryar Filsun lays down a thin blanket, and we sit. Zahra stands before us, watching the boys run off with the ball. She walks after them slowly, keeping a distance. When the ball rolls by her, she's quick to pick up the skirt of her abaya and handle the ball, stopping it, positioning it, and passing it deftly to Abdi-Nur, who has his hands on his hips, dejected. He rolls the ball farther along the beach away from her, and the other boys run after him. Zahra comes back towards us and sits down. Habaryar Filsun is on the phone.

I look in my wallet. I have forty dirhams. "Come on," I say to Zahra, getting up.

When Habaryar Filsun asks us where we're going, I point to the Pizza Hut. She hands me a five-dirham bill and makes a drinking gesture with her free hand. I nod and we walk across the sand, sinking with each step.

"Wouldn't let you play, huh?" I say. I mean to be sympathetic but it sounds teasing.

Zahra doesn't respond for a moment. "It's because I'm better than them," she says.

"And because you're a girl," I add. I hold open the Pizza Hut door. "My little Cinderella." Zahra looks bewildered. "Should we get a pizza? A small one? I'm not very hungry, but look," I say, pointing at the sign. "We can get a small and share?"

"Yeah, okay."

We take our order outside and find a picnic table that's just being left by a young Indian couple with a stroller and two small children. The wife smiles at us as she cleans up the table.

"Why did you call me Cinderella?" Zahra asks, taking a seat.

"What?"

"You called me Cinderella just now."

"Oh," I say, ripping the crust off my pizza slice. "It was a joke." I start eating.

Zahra stares at me. She hasn't taken a bite of the slice she's holding.

"Cinderella is a princess. It's really a compliment," I say, covering my mouth with the back of my hand.

"She was practically a slave," Zahra says pointedly.

"Yeah," I say, buying time as I chew, "but...then... after...she became a princess."

Zahra withdraws, and I wish I had never said it.

Over the next few days, when her mother calls for her, she moves slowly or puts a pillow over her head and pretends to be asleep. I make excuses for her, telling Habaryar Filsun she has a headache or is taking a nap. She shoots dirty looks at Abdi-Nur when he talks to her, which he lets go after mumbling about how weird or dumb she is. She usually ignores him, but once, she flippantly tells him to shut up in a biting tone that makes Abdi-Majid and Abdi-Karim burst out laughing. Zahra snickers, pleased with herself, and I have to placate Abdi-Nur when he gets in her face, prepared to hit her, all the while hoping that Habaryar Filsun doesn't hear what's going on from her bedroom. I can't help but feel like I'm responsible, so I try to pick up Zahra's slack, helping Habaryar clear the table and load the dishwasher. I'm leaving in a few days, and I'm troubled by what might happen once I'm gone.

The night after the squabble between Zahra and Abdi-Nur, I take a long, hot shower. I put on a clean baati and wrap my hair in a microfibre towel. When I go into the bedroom, Zahra is lying in bed, reading.

I sit on the bed nervously. "Zahra," I say. "Are you all right?"

"Mhmm," she says, turning a page.

After a few minutes, she picks up her bookmark from the nightstand and closes the book, leaving it sitting on her chest. "Can I ask you something?"

"Yeah, sure." I push myself back on the bed so I can lean against the wall.

"Is it true?"

"Is what true?"

"About...the jinn?" She looks both eager and apprehensive.

"Oh." It's not that I'm offended. I just wonder how to explain it, since no one has asked me before. "No, it's not true."

She looks at me as though deciding whether to believe me.

"Have you ever had the urge to scream?" I ask cautiously.

"To scream?"

"Yeah."

She shakes her head.

"Hm," I say. "Well, you might not understand but... ever since I was little, I don't know why...but, there would be times when I just wanted to scream." I stop to gauge her reaction. She seems interested. "I'd be in class or on the bus or something, and I'd think—I would just wonder—what if I screamed right now? Like, what would happen? Would someone call the police? Would they ask me what's wrong?

Of course, I never did it, because that's crazy, right? To just scream in public for no reason.

"But then it was like everything started to go wrong. I got fired from my job. It was a stupid call centre job, but still. I fought with my supervisor because I was always late. I just didn't care. And then I failed my nursing exam for the last time. You only get three chances and . . . well. So I can't be a nurse. And I've been studying for years. And I really tried." I shrug. "Anyway, that was bad enough. But then my . . . my best friend—her name is Najma—well, she was my best friend. I fought with her, too."

I shake my head and have a fleeting thought that I am sharing way too much with Zahra, who is, after all, only twelve. But I have to keep going. I have to explain all of it to at least one person.

"So I thought, I have no job. I have no friends. I have no future. *This is the perfect time to scream.*" Zahra's book has slid off her chest and fallen to the floor. She doesn't pick it up. "So I screamed," I say nonchalantly. "And, you know, it's funny, because screaming is one of those things that is really difficult to stop once you start. I just kept screaming. My mom didn't know what to do. My brother was trying everything to calm me down. He looked terrified." I give a little laugh. "But I just thought, let me get it all out, you know? All of those times that I wanted to scream and didn't. Let me do it now."

Zahra sits up and crosses her legs underneath her. "So what happened?" she says faintly.

I stare at her as if it's obvious. "They put me in the goddamn hospital, that's what happened! They thought I was possessed. First, Hooya dragged me to the masjid for Quran saar, but I didn't improve, so . . ."

"Ohhh."

"Psychiatric evaluation." I say the words slowly. "Three days." I drop my hands onto my thighs, which makes a clapping noise. "But you know Somalis. They don't understand mental health. I had a *breakdown*. That's what my doctor said. Due to all of the stresses in my life. He put me on antidepressants."

"Is it?" Zahra says compassionately. "Mum said it was a jinn."

I shake my head. "That's easier for them to believe. It's easier to blame your problems on some unpredictable, otherworldly power beyond our control, you know?" I fall silent, moved by my own words. "Not that jinns aren't real," I quickly add. "It's just, in *my* case, it wasn't that."

Zahra is quiet for a while. She leans back against the headboard, pulling a pillow from behind her to hold in her arms. "You screamed? That's it?" She looks at me, and her gaze is so strong that, for a moment, I'm daunted. Then I understand—

"No, no, wait!" I say, as her mouth stretches open, but it's too late.

Zahra screams so loud that I have to cover my ears. Her scream is high-pitched and sharp. It sounds like she's experiencing incredible physical pain, but she's sitting perfectly still in her bed. Within seconds, Habaryar Filsun and the boys are crowding the room, shouting, demanding to know what's happened. I stand up, unsure how to explain. Zahra keeps shrieking, her head cocked back, even when her mother shakes her, even after Abdi-Majid, the baby of the family, backs out of the room. Then Zahra stops and clears her throat. Everyone is quiet, and Habaryar Filsun's eyes are filled with tears. I almost feel sorry when Zahra points her finger at them and laughs and laughs and laughs until she can't catch her breath.

Toronto, 2020

ON THE SECOND DAY of the new year, Jihan became increasingly aware of a persistent pain in her stomach. She had the urge to expel the pain from her body. She threw up. She sat on the toilet, clutching her abdomen. Finally, she called her father, who was driving his taxi, to pick her up and take her to the emergency room. He wanted to take her to Sunnybrook since it was close by, but she insisted on North York General Hospital because it was newer, and she had the idea that the emergency room would be less crowded.

Jihan called her mother, who was on the Leon's furniture showroom floor, getting the knots in her back worked out in a massage chair while her friend deliberated between two dining room sets. Sounding uneasy, Jihan's mother offered to meet her, but Jihan told her not to bother; she was still in the waiting room.

She waited for an hour and a half. Then Jihan's name was called and she was escorted through sliding doors into another mini waiting room where an indifferent nurse asked her some questions. Her blood was taken. She was told to follow another nurse, a young, hardy-looking East Asian woman who was chewing gum. Jihan walked down long halls, through doors, went up in an elevator, into a change room where she put on a hospital gown and re-secured her hijab, and finally, into a room for an abdominal ultrasound. She began to fear a serious diagnosis — like lupus or cancer — and tried to read the technician's face for clues, but the technician revealed nothing and only directed her back to the change room. It was there in the corridor, distracted by her anxiety, holding the loose fabric of the hospital gown close to her body for fear of exposure, that she saw — passing swiftly in a wheelchair that was being pushed by a bulky male nurse — the unmistakable profile of Bilal Dire. His head was shaved and partly bandaged. He looked smaller, thinner. Jihan's whole body turned as she watched the wheelchair glide across the tiled floor and enter an elevator, where the nurse adroitly turned it 180 degrees so that Bilal was facing out, staring right at her. The elevator doors closed slowly.

Jihan loosened her grip on the fabric of the hospital gown and dropped her hands. The pain in her side no longer consumed her. She walked with tiny steps, disoriented, unsure where the change room had been. A nurse with a clipboard touched her shoulder and asked what she was looking for. Jihan took a deep breath. "I'm okay," she said. It was impossible. She was hallucinating. She had conjured him out of some subconscious desire to see him again. Or perhaps it was the fear of death. The fear of the doctors very soon being able to assess what was ailing her and, after sending her to some specialists, estimate how long she would have to live. And her mind had jumped to the most recent reference to death she had: five days earlier, Bilal had left his house and walked to his car in the parking lot, and then seconds later, the driver's side window was blown out, and Bilal was slumped over the emergency brake and centre console.

IT WAS APPENDICITIS. The doctor, a lean, middle-aged Ghanaian man, praised Jihan for recognizing the signals her body was sending her. He told the student doctor next to him that women were better at recognizing pain and not expecting it to resolve itself. The infection was in its early stages, so the doctor gave Jihan the option of treating it with antibiotics or scheduling the appendectomy if the pain was too severe. Jihan chose the pills, and he smiled, nodded, and squeezed her upper arm. He watched the student doctor administer morphine to Jihan through an IV and wrote her a prescription.

In a daze, she waited for her father to pick her up. He took her to fill her prescription at the Shoppers Drug Mart on Lawrence Avenue West and Dufferin, and then dropped her off at home before driving off to finish his shift. Jihan drifted into a deep sleep. She saw herself clutching at the hospital gown that inadequately covered her, as Bilal rolled by in a wheelchair. This time, there was no nurse pushing him. The wheelchair was gliding along the hard floor on its own. The elevator doors opened and the chair turned itself around and backed inside. Bilal, from fifteen metres away, looked straight into Jihan's eyes, as if to say, *I know you saw me, but who will believe you?*

Jihan woke with a start to find her mother hovering over her. Her mother reached for the prescription bottle on the stool by Jihan's bed and asked her how she was feeling, what the doctor had said, and what the pills were for. She bustled out of the room to make Jihan some vegetable soup, her wide hips nearly knocking over the floor lamp by the door. Jihan was comforted. It was easy for her, in that moment, to blur both scenes together so that they became the hazy recollections of a dream. She reached under her pillow for her iPhone and searched Bilal's name on Google. The first four links were purple — stories she had already read. She clicked on the first one. The CP24 local news story was headlined:

YOUNG MAN GUNNED DOWN IN LAWRENCE HEIGHTS
WAS KNOWN TO POLICE

Jihan scrolled down to the picture, which, surprisingly, wasn't a mug shot. Instead, Bilal leaned against the hood of a white Acura TLX, his arms crossed in a grey Champion sweatshirt. Jihan zoomed in. She could see Bilal's dimples. His thick, matted curls that he grew out. His skin was dark and perfectly even, his eyelashes long, his jaw definite.

Under the photo, in small font:

Bilal Dire, 18, was murdered on December 28, 2019. Police are still investigating.

He was dead. Jihan had accompanied her mother to the tacsi. They had crossed the street from their apartment building to the row of townhouses where Bilal lived. They had brought a twenty-four-pack of bottled water and a twelve-pack of Coca-Cola. She had stood in Habaryar Yasmin's living room with a crowd of women until Hafsa, who lived three houses down, motioned for her to come to the basement, where some of the other neighbourhood kids were sitting solemnly. Two days later, Jihan went to Bilal's Janazah, even though she was on her period and couldn't join the funeral prayer. All she could do was sit at the back of the masjid by herself and make dua for him.

~

THE WINTER TERM BEGAN. Jihan sat in a lecture hall in the Vanier building at York University, her laptop, notebook, and pencil case neatly arranged in front of her. She tried to focus on the professor at the front of the room, and guess at whether she would like her by the end of the course. When the class was over, Jihan stayed seated until students for the next class started to file in. Then she got up, mechanically. She was hungry, but she wouldn't eat. She walked to the train station and bumped into Hafsa, who was late for a tutorial.

"You're heading home already? I'm so jealous," Hafsa said, rushing off.

But Jihan was not heading home. She took the train and a bus, and then rode the train again until she was standing in front of the information desk in the lobby of the North York General Hospital. Hesitantly, she approached the receptionist and told her she was looking for a patient. When she was asked for a name, Jihan said, "Bilal Dire. B-I-L-A-L D-I-R-E. Bilal Dire."

The woman typed rapidly at the keyboard and shook her head. "No one by that name. Try Sunnybrook."

She was so matter-of-fact that Jihan was too daunted to ask her to verify the spelling. Instead, she backed away to let the family behind her approach the desk. A grey-haired man in a lumberjack sweater was holding a bouquet of helium balloons, one of which announced: IT'S A BOY!

Jihan felt light-headed. She hadn't eaten since breakfast and feared what might happen if she tried to venture back home on an empty stomach. She found a Subway in a food court past the information desk. Precisely at the moment she had taken the last bite of her six-inch tuna melt, she saw two middle-aged Somali women hurrying past. They looked familiar to her in the way that all Somali women looked familiar to her, and although they were not from her neighbourhood, Jihan jumped up to throw out the sandwich wrapping, wiped at her mouth with a napkin, and intuitively followed them.

As the women waited for the elevator, Jihan hung back and some hospital staff gathered around, shielding her from view. They all entered the elevator together, Jihan slipping to the back. A doctor in a white coat pressed the button for the sixth floor. One of the women said, "Is that right?" in Somali, and the other mumbled, "Yes, yes. But we don't have much time." They were the first to get off on the sixth floor. The doctor and nurses also got off. Jihan was last. She kept her eyes on the women. They walked with resolve, past a large desk with nurses who paid them no mind. They took a right. Jihan saw signs for the Intensive Care Unit. Finally, they stopped in front of an open door, looked in, and declared that it was the next one.

Jihan exhaled. As she approached the next room, she noticed a window before the door, blinds drawn. The blinds were bent in some places, so Jihan could see inside, but the two women were blocking her view of the patient. Instead, she saw a young woman in her mid- to late twenties sitting limply in an armchair in the corner. She had prominent dark circles around her large eyes, and the orange scarf tied around her head turban-style was coming undone. When one of the visitors moved towards her to hold her hand, Jihan could see a boy of about four, eyes closed, hooked up to countless machines, lying still on the hospital bed.

Jihan felt a weight of sadness merge with her confusion. She was tired. She wanted to go home. Yet her eyes continued to frantically search each room she passed until she spotted—spread open and held at precisely the right height to obscure the patient's face—the book *Black Panther: A Nation under Our Feet* by Ta-Nehisi Coates.

Jihan stopped at the door. "Bilal?"

The patient didn't respond. Didn't move.

"Bilal, is that you?" she said as she approached. Jihan quickly studied the hands that held the book: black, large, veined . . . They were the hands of a young man. But the patient remained silent and moved the book closer to their face the nearer she got, as if, no matter how obviously, they were determined to hide from her view.

"Bilal," she said, almost a cry.

She pushed the book down, surprised that she could do it so easily. At last, his face emerged, with a grin that revealed both defeat and approval.

"You got me," said Bilal.

"YOU'RE REALLY ALIVE."

Bilal closed the book and laid it beside him. "It's complicated."

Jihan stood there staring at him for what felt like minutes. She could not move.

Bilal shifted in the hospital bed, sitting up straighter as she stared. Finally, he broke the silence. "Why don't you sit down?" He pointed to a chair in the corner of the room.

Jihan shook her head; she refused to take her eyes off him. She dropped her backpack and sat on the edge of the bed. "Everyone thinks you're dead," she said, her tone lowered.

"I know."

"I went to your Janazah."

After a pause, "How was it?"

"Bilal... what's going on? I'm scared." Jihan felt her nose become hot. She feared the tears that were coming and fought them.

Bilal sighed. "Listen, I can't say much. You can't tell anyone. You understand that, right?"

Jihan nodded.

"I mean, not even my mother. It's very important. Promise me."

"Okay. But why?"

"Close the door."

Jihan walked backwards to the door and pushed it closed gently. She took her place again at the end of the bed and waited. When Bilal looked like he was about to speak, she interrupted him: "What about your injuries?"

Although Bilal was in a private room in the Intensive Care Unit, there seemed to be nothing but a heart rate monitor attached to him. The bandage she had noticed wrapped around his head a few days ago was gone, and Jihan could see a long incision starting from his left ear, which was held closed with a pattern of black stitches. He told her a bullet had passed through the left side of his brain. Part of his skull was removed to allow the brain to swell. Apparently, he spoke to the doctors throughout the nine-hour surgery. Bilal exposed his bandaged left shoulder, where he had also been struck. The third bullet had missed him.

"Do you know who it was?" He asked Jihan, his eyes piercing hers.

"I've heard things, but I don't know for sure."

Bilal nodded. "What things? Tell me. What did you hear?"

"You didn't see anything?"

"It happened so fast," he said. "I got in my car. I was about to push the start button. Then I heard a bang."

Jihan felt such pity for him. Their neighbourhood was known as "Jungle"—and it was just that. Subsidized townhouses and apartment buildings were clustered along the intersecting network of small roads in Lawrence Heights. Jihan could count on one hand the number of fatal shootings that had happened in broad daylight since she had moved there with her parents in the seventh grade. Within hours, the whole neighbourhood would learn some version of the events, just enough to satisfy their curiosity, to comfort them with the knowledge that the attack was targeted, not random, and that they were relatively safe so long as they minded their business and used common sense. But when Jihan heard about what had happened to Bilal, she felt sick. She didn't want to know any details about the shooting besides who was responsible.

She hated the gossip. On the fourth day of the tacsi, Jihan had been sitting in Habaryar Yasmin's basement with some girls from the neighbourhood. With self-righteous piety, one of them said something about the consequences of being a drug dealer, as though Bilal's death should be a lesson to them all. Years before, Jihan had been friends with the girl, but they had naturally drifted apart, and more recently, the girl had become religious. Now, they only stopped to say hello if they ran into each other on the street or at Lawrence West station.

"*You're* talking?" Jihan exclaimed. "*You?* You're banned from Yorkdale. You spent high school shoplifting from Zara. And *you're* talking?"

There was an audible gasp, and some girls snickered before the room fell into a stifling silence. The girl, who was already light-skinned and even paler because it was winter, flushed red with humiliation. Her mouth hung open, but she didn't say a word.

What could Jihan tell Bilal? How could she even begin to explain what little she had the stomach to listen to? "I don't know much. The police are still investigating," she offered.

He looked at her, his eyes narrowing. He had not seen the gunman who was lying in wait for him, and this, to Jihan, seemed like a mercy. She felt apologetic, and guilty, but she could not bring herself to tell Bilal what had happened to him. The idea mortified her.

"Find out for me. You can find out, right?"

She nodded vaguely, just as a nurse entered the room. Visiting hours were over, and it was time for Bilal's medication. Jihan pulled her phone out of her pocket and saw that it was ten to five.

"Okay," she said, standing up. "It's okay. I'll come back tomorrow." She picked up her backpack. "We'll talk more tomorrow."

"Jihan," Bilal said gravely, "you can't tell anyone."

"I won't. Wallahi."

She said goodbye and made note of Bilal's room number. She turned around in the hall to look in on him one more time and saw him lying with his arms folded across his chest, staring up at the ceiling, an expression of absolute repose on his face.

That look unsettled her, because only moments before, Bilal had been so confused, so lost. He was insulated from the events that followed his attack: the immediate spectacle that drew neighbours out of their homes, the procession of emergency vehicles that slowly made their way down Flemington Avenue, his funeral, and the sporadic news reporting on his case. But Bilal wanted answers, and the more Jihan deliberated, the more she understood that he was owed the truth.

Everyone said the shooter was S. J. — a seventeen-year-old boy who had grown up in Jihan's very own building, raised by his grandmother. Jihan thought back to all the times she had seen S. J. in the lobby or elevators. He was small, no taller than five six. A quiet, brooding boy with a large gap between his front teeth. In the aftermath of Bilal's murder, S. J.'s absence was glaring. Jihan had not seen him huddled outside of Bilal's house with the other boys who had stopped by to give their brief condolences to Habaryar Yasmin. She had not seen him outside of the mosque, walking to his family car in a thobe and Timberland boots or arranging a ride with others who were headed to the cemetery for the burial. She even asked her father if he had seen S. J. on the men's side during the Janazah prayer, and he said he hadn't. S. J. was no longer in the neighbourhood; Jihan was sure of it. He was on the run.

She phoned Nabila that night. Nabila's family had moved out of Jungle years before, after buying a house in Markham. She had four brothers, one of whom—Guled—had been best friends with Bilal and had volunteered to wash Bilal's body for the funeral rites. Jihan had seen Nabila inside the mosque, but the crowd of worshippers pushed them along, so they could only pass each other, reach out a hand, and squeeze, expressing with their eyes a hope to find each other outside once the Janazah was over. Jihan was struck by Nabila's changed appearance—her ashy face, her dry lips. Grief had made her ugly. She knew that Bilal was like a fifth brother to Nabila, and since Jihan had no brothers, she surmised that Nabila's pain was different from her own.

They exchanged pleasantries and made small talk. Finally, Jihan came out with it: "Why did S. J. do it?" she asked. "I mean, what was the reason?"

"It's so stupid." Jihan could hear the exasperation in Nabila's voice. "It was about a hammer."

~

THE NEXT MORNING, Jihan met Hafsa at the bus stop. They commuted together on Wednesdays to the same third-year Women in Anthropology course. While they waited for the bus, Jihan shared what she had heard from Nabila. Hafsa listened attentively, nodding along, until she heard the part about the gun and stuck out her gloved hand, forcing Jihan to stop.

"Wait, wait. I thought it was over a robbery," Hafsa said. "A robbery gone wrong or something."

"Maybe they were stealing guns?"

"To sell?"

"I don't know."

"I heard it was over a robbery. Like Bilal didn't give S. J. his cut of something."

"Where'd you hear that?" Jihan asked.

"I can't remember." Hafsa shrugged and got on the bus. It was full so they both had to stand.

Hafsa seemed deep in thought. She stared out of the window while she gripped the handrail. "I thought you didn't like talking about this," she said, glancing at Jihan.

"About Bilal?"

"Yeah. Did you like him or something?"

Jihan braced for a stop, steadying herself. "What?"

"Don't play dumb. Did you like him?"

They trailed off the bus and into Lawrence West Station.

"He's two years younger than me," Jihan said.

"So? He was cute."

Jihan knew what Hafsa was doing. She was goading her in the unique, preternatural way of girls—seemingly detached while searching intensely for data. But Bilal had always been one of the boys from her neighbourhood. Jihan had never paid any special attention to him until her last year of high school, when she had found herself roaming empty halls after writing a makeup test after school. She was standing at the front doors, watching fat flakes fall upon the snow-covered ground, regretting her decision to spend her change on a poutine instead of saving it for bus fare, when Bilal walked through the doors.

"What are you doing here?" she asked. It was a Friday.

"I forgot something," he said, pointing in the direction of the east wing, where his locker was. He moved to walk off.

"Hey," she said, "do you have an extra bus token?" She became a little shy. "I was gonna walk, but the weather looks bad."

He half smiled, his dimples appearing. "Yeah, it's pretty bad. Here," he said, digging in his pocket and handing her two toonies.

From that moment on, she did like him. She thought he was kind and generous and easygoing. But Bilal was still a kid. Jihan wondered how he would turn out in three or four years. Maybe she would really like him then.

"I guess I just don't understand," Jihan said. "I can't believe it."

Hafsa's eyes lit up. "Oh! I just remembered, my mom said a silver s u v almost ran into Mrs. Owens that day when she was crossing Varna. She was coming off work. Almost killed her."

"A silver s u v?"

"Uh-huh."

"So?"

"So? It was obviously the getaway car. You don't think that kid acted alone, do you?"

Jihan dropped the subject. She had wanted to gather what information she could for Bilal, but Hafsa was already suspicious.

After class, Jihan began the journey to the hospital, attempting to read the first chapter of Frantz Fanon's *The Wretched of the Earth*. She found herself skimming repeatedly over the same passage: "Confronted with a world configured by the colonizer, the colonized subject is always presumed guilty. The colonized does not accept his guilt, but rather considers it a kind of curse."

When she arrived, Bilal was sitting in the armchair in his room, next to a tray on a table with wheels. Jihan sighed in relief. She hung her coat on a hook behind the door and sat on the edge of the bed.

"How are you?" she asked.

Bilal was eating applesauce with a plastic spoon. "I'm all right."

He looked a little stronger, more assured. She could see his legs from under his hospital gown. His knees were scarred, his shins hairy.

"So...I asked around about that thing you wanted to know."

Bilal just looked at her expectantly.

"It was S. J."

Bilal nodded his head very slowly. He seemed resigned.

Jihan carried on. "Apparently, just after it happened, a silver suv almost crashed into an old lady who was walking home."

"Hm."

"That could've been the getaway car. I mean, no one's seen S. J. since. He's definitely hiding out."

"Thanks," Bilal said, his expression pained.

Jihan understood that he didn't want to hear any more, so she said nothing about the gun or the theories about a robbery. Bilal pushed the table away and into the wall and leaned back in his chair.

They were both quiet for a while.

"Can I ask you something?" Jihan said. "How did you manage to...survive? I still don't understand."

Bilal seemed to be searching for the right words. Finally, he said, "I played dead."

"You played dead?"

"Yeah. I slumped over, and I listened, but I didn't hear nothing. So I called the ambulance."

"You called the ambulance yourself?"

"Yeah. No one came out for minutes. I could have died."

"So when the ambulance came, you still played dead?"

"It took them a while to come. The neighbours started peeking around by then. I could hear them stepping on glass. I heard my mom screaming. It was really hard, but I had to do it. I just knew I couldn't move. I couldn't breathe. I had to act dead."

"But why? S. J. was long gone by then."

He raised his eyebrows and frowned slightly, as if to say he didn't have an explanation.

"What about in the ambulance?"

Bilal sighed. "I heard them say, 'He's dead.' But I wasn't."

"What did you do?"

"I wanted to keep playing dead, but I thought I might *actually* die. So I moved my finger, and they could see I was alive. They tried to stop the bleeding from my head and my shoulder. They drove faster. They took me to Sunnybrook."

"And you had surgery?"

"Yeah, and then they transferred me here."

"So . . ." Jihan was lost for words. "Why did they say you died?"

Bilal cleared his throat. "I — I don't know."

169

"Bilal—" Jihan almost laughed but caught herself. "That doesn't make any sense." He was quiet, so she continued. "I told you. There was a whole funeral—"

"Why do you care so much? Shit! Leave me alone!" His words merged in a furious outburst.

Jihan was baffled, a sharp pain in her chest. She scooted off the bed, picked up her bag and coat, and walked out of the room. In the hallway, she forced herself to sit on a bench and close her eyes. She didn't expect Bilal to snap at her when she was only trying to understand, to explain how everyone had mourned his death. But Bilal seemed totally removed from everyone, including his family. His poor mother looked like she had no energy to care for the young children from her second marriage. Didn't he owe her something? How could he let her go on believing he was dead? Jihan went home, unable to read Fanon, her eyes wandering over the words but grasping nothing.

She took a shower, heated up the beef stew her mother had cooked, and ripped half of a piece of Ethiopian injera that was sitting in a bag on the table. She ate slowly, washed up, and took a can of Coke out of the fridge. She closed the door to her room and sat at her desk. She wanted to get an early start on the first assignment for her Poli-Sci course—a case study on a developing country, paying specific atten- tion to significant events occurring post-colonialism. She had to choose from a list of ten countries and settled on

Zimbabwe, reasoning that the 2017 coup and resignation of Mugabe would give her ample material. She googled Mugabe. His face appeared, tight-lipped and stern, with his thinning hair and the shining pin on his suit lapel. He *looked* like a dictator. Jihan typed *Paul Kagame*. She clicked on a photo of him seated, the tips of his fingers joined, the thick-framed glasses, the slightly red eyes. Behind him and on his lapel pin was the Rwandan flag, the rays of its yellow sun expanding. She wished she could do her case study on Rwanda so she could highlight the glowing success of an African nation after a brutal civil war, rather than hand in a timeline of oppression and failures to her Latin American professor. She closed her browser and stared at the expanse of white in front of her. She wrote:

CASE STUDY: ZIMBABWE

She began to cry.

BILAL HAD MADE HIMSELF CLEAR: he didn't want to be found. He had humoured Jihan out of necessity. She was a relic of his past. Not distinct or important enough to carry forward into whatever future he had imagined for himself, but not insignificant enough to ignore when she had appeared before him.

Then, a few nights later, she heard her mother on the phone, talking loudly about how S. J. had been arrested in Montreal. Although she was apprehensive about visiting Bilal again, Jihan headed to the hospital the next morning to tell him the news. Relaying the message about S. J.'s arrest would give her an opportunity to smooth things over.

Standing in the doorway to Bilal's room, Jihan's heart dropped. An old man now occupied the bed. He seemed to be unconscious, an oxygen mask secured to his face while he lay still. Jihan spotted the nurse who had told her visiting hours were over. She asked her about Bilal, but the woman looked puzzled, mumbled about the front desk, and walked away.

Jihan wandered down the hall until she came upon the room where she had seen the sick little Somali boy and his worried mother. The room was vacant and being cleaned by hospital staff.

Discouraged, Jihan got into the elevator to leave, but when the doors opened at the first floor, Bilal was standing in front of her with a Subway sandwich in his hand. She barrelled towards him, and then caught herself, stopping just in front of him. He gazed down at her.

"I thought you were gone!"

Bilal nodded towards the elevator and hit the button for the second floor. "I'm in the general ward now."

He led her to a large room with four beds and two other patients. One was a middle-aged man who was asleep. The other was reading the *Toronto Star*.

"Thanks, brother," Bilal said, holding up his sub to the man reading the paper. "He bought me lunch," he said to Jihan. "Do you want the bed or the chair?"

Jihan shrugged. "It doesn't matter."

Bilal took the chair, setting his sandwich down. "I'm sick of hospital beds."

Jihan sat on the bed. "Is it okay to talk?"

"Yeah. Don't mind them, they're cool."

Jihan looked around. "S. J. was arrested in Montreal yesterday."

Bilal looked up from unwrapping his sub, but he made no comment.

"That's good news, right?" she said.

"Good news for who? Not for him."

"For you."

Bilal tilted his head. "I don't know. I'm starting to think it has nothing to do with me."

Jihan stared at him, perplexed. Then she thought she understood his meaning. "You're right. I can't figure out what he's been charged with. There's barely any information."

Bilal took a huge bite of his sandwich. Jihan was sorry that she was forcing an interaction he did not wish to partake in — that she had inserted herself into his life once again. But she had just arrived. She thought leaving already would highlight her awkwardness even more. So Jihan sat there while Bilal ate his sub.

"What are you going to do?" she asked.

"What do you mean?"

"I mean, when you get out of here. What are you going to do?"

He wiped his mouth with a napkin and crumpled the wrapping into a small ball. "I'm gonna go home."

"To Jungle?"

"No." He threw the bag in the wastebasket by the bed. "Back home. Home-home."

Jihan couldn't hide her surprise. "You were born here, right?"

"Uh-huh."

"Have you ever been back home?"

"No."

"So . . . you're gonna go back home? By yourself?"

He nodded. "That's the plan."

"Hm."

"What? You don't think it's a good idea?"

"It's dangerous. Unless you're planning on living in Hargeisa or something."

"It's dangerous here. For me, at least."

He had a point, but Jihan couldn't tell if he was being

serious. How would it work? How was he—a young man who had been born and raised in Toronto—going to make a life in a country that was, for all intents and purposes, completely foreign to him? It seemed naive to Jihan, but she was tired of pestering him. "I'm sure you'll figure it out," she said, trying for an optimistic tone.

There seemed to be nothing more to say, yet Jihan delayed getting up. She knew she would never see Bilal again. He was recovering quickly. His hair was growing in. He looked more and more out of place in the hospital that surrounded him.

Finally, she rose. "I'll pray for you."

"Thank you. I need it," he said.

Jihan picked up her bag and waved at him as she walked out of the room.

She was walking across the lobby, trying to imagine Bilal back home—in Gaalkayo or Baidoa or Kismaayo— when she felt something crash against her boot. She looked down to see the little Somali boy from the Intensive Care Unit reaching for a toy fire truck that had landed at her feet. The boy looked happy and robust in his yellow padded coat.

Jihan smiled. "Mashallah! He's so much better!"

The boy's mother approached and smiled back awkwardly. "I'm sorry." She seemed to be studying Jihan. "Do I know you?"

"My friend Bilal Dire spent some time on the same floor as you," Jihan explained.

"Bilal Dire? Why does that name sound familiar?" The boy's mother mulled it over for a moment, and then her eyes sparked with recognition. "Bilal Dire. Isn't that the kid from the news? No—never mind. The person I'm thinking of was killed. Really sad." Her eyes searched for her son, who had wandered a few feet away with his truck. "I hope your friend is doing better," she said, as she chased after her boy.

Jihan's body tensed up as if she were frozen in place. In her mind, Bilal stood tall, an expanse of dusty land behind him. She wondered hopelessly if, in a few years, she might accompany her mother back home and bump into him. If one day, while at a market in Hamar, she might notice the intricate scar on the shoulder of a sleeveless fruit seller and look up to see Bilal's dimpled face.

But she knew her life would never lead her to that future.

Acknowledgements

FIRST AND FOREMOST, I would like to thank Allah, the most high, who has blessed me in more ways than I can count.

Thank you to the Canada Council for the Arts for providing me with the funding to complete this collection.

I would like to thank my editor, Shirarose Wilensky, for not only understanding my vision for this collection, but for helping me achieve that vision with her incredible taste and eye for detail! Thank you to the whole team at House of Anansi, including Jenny McWha and Emilia Morgan. I am very grateful to the cover designer, Alysia Shewchuk.

Thank you to the University of Guelph's M.F.A program. Over the years, I have had the privilege of studying the craft of writing with some of Canada's best writers. Each one has inspired me, enriched me, and ultimately encouraged me to keep going. I would like to thank Michael Helm, Catherine Bush, Russell Smith, Madeleine Thien (an extra thank you for your kind words and support!), Michael Winter, Marni Jackson, and Dionne Brand.

I would like to thank my friends Linzey Corridon and Samantha Barry for their constant support during this process! A special thank you to Canisia Lubrin for all her help! I would also like to thank Victoria Hall, who published an earlier version of "Toronto, 2011" as "Sticking Together" in *Emotional Magazine*. I would like to express my gratitude to the editors of *Brick* for publishing "Amsterdam, 2008."

Thanks to my brother Kalid, for pushing me to publish! Finally, I would like to thank my mother for her unending sacrifice, her strength, and her wisdom, but mostly for being my mother.

Eluvier Acosta

IDMAN NUR OMAR was born in Rome and immigrated to Canada in 1991. She has an M.F.A. in creative writing from the University of Guelph and an M.A. in English Literature from Concordia University. She lives in Calgary, where she teaches at the Southern Alberta Institute of Technology in the Communication and Liberal Arts Studies Department.